*Journey of a Lifetime
and Other Stories*

BY THE SAME AUTHOR

Fiction
Someone Else
Fly Away Home
Dances of Death: Short Stories
The Traveller and His Child
The China Egg and Other Stories
The Intruder
Looking Forward
To the City
Give Them All My Love

Non-fiction
The Born Exile: George Gissing
The Fields Beneath: The History of One London Village
City of Gold: The Biography of Bombay
Rosamond Lehmann: An Appreciation

JOURNEY OF A LIFETIME

and Other Stories

Gillian Tindall

HUTCHINSON
LONDON SYDNEY AUCKLAND JOHANNESBURG

This edition first published in Great Britain
by Hutchinson, an imprint of Century Hutchinson Ltd,
20 Vauxhall Bridge Road,
London SW1V 2SA

Century Hutchinson (Australia) Pty Ltd
20 Alfred Street, Milsons Point, Sydney,
NSW 2061, Australia

Century Hutchinson New Zealand Ltd
PO Box 40–086, Glenfield, Auckland 10, New Zealand

Century Hutchinson South Africa (Pty) Ltd
PO Box 337, Bergvlei, 2102 South Africa

British Library Cataloguing in Publication Data
Tindall, Gillian, 1938–
    Journey of a Lifetime and other stories.
    I. Title
    823'.914 [F]

    ISBN 0–09–174450–4

Photoset by Deltatype Ltd, Ellesmere Port, Cheshire
Printed and bound by Butler & Tanner Ltd, Frome, Somerset

Contents

Some of these stories have previously appeared in *The London Magazine, Encounter, Woman's Journal, The Illustrated Weekly of India* and *Winter's Tales*, and one has been read on the BBC.

Journey of a Lifetime

She was packing to go away, not just for a holiday this time
but for a long while: there was so much still to do.
Distractedly she filled suitcases with her own clothes and
her husband's; she had said that she would pack for him, as
he would be busy at work; then they could leave in the
evening as soon as he got home. But she kept remembering
more things that must go in, not just isolated objects but
whole ranges of things, whole departments of life. And not
only things that needed packing but other matters that
should be attended to in different ways: the gas, the
electricity, stuff at the cleaners . . . and what about the
cats? What arrangements had she made about them?

The usual one, surely, but she could not be certain – and
there was so little time . . . She looked at her watch. The
afternoon was rapidly passing. She suddenly knew that she
ought to put polythene sheets over the furniture as well.
And go and see their neighbour before leaving. And the
jobbing gardener . . . And were there outstanding bills to
pay?

But what really distracted her, preventing her from
concentrating on the packing while yet making it impera-
tive that she should get it done *now*, without further muddle
or delay, was the awful knowledge that she had not yet got
the plane tickets. She surely should have done? It must have
been her responsibility, and her husband would be relying
on her having done so with her usual competence. Or no –
wait: did he perhaps have his own ticket already, as he
sometimes did, provided by the firm? If so, it was just her
ticket that she had, idiotically, failed to order. She had
certainly meant to.

Six o'clock. That was when their travel agent closed.
(Her busy life was organised upon a series of fixed props:
'their' travel agent, jobbing gardener, carpenter, plumber,

locksmith, cleaner, neighbour, little-man-round-the-corner, grocer-who-delivers.) The travel agent was so helpful, if only she could get down to him before six all might yet be well. But further suspicion nagged: when did the plane actually leave? Much later than six? Possibly. But they would still have to get out to the airport . . .

She realised that she had yet to wash her hair. And she must wash it. It was, for some reason, crawling with insects and coming out in handfuls. The strands disintegrated between her fingers with a nameless corruption. She tried to scream, but no sound came.

She woke. Relief seeped through her. It was not late afternoon but early in the morning. She had the whole day to do things, and her husband would do his share; he was not going to work. He was asleep beside her now, and in fact he would not be going to work any more on a regular basis ever again, as he had recently retired. That was the reason they were able to make this extended trip: months and months slowly encircling the world in modest, economical stages, staying with this old friend here, looking up that erstwhile work-contact there. It was going to be the journey of a lifetime.

And of course she hadn't failed to pick up the tickets. They were all there, a whole folder of them, along with the passports, visas, health certificates and other necessary papers, sitting safe in the desk drawer, and had been for the last fortnight.

'I had a ghastly dream,' she said to her husband when he stirred. 'I'm so glad to wake up.'

'What dream?' he said dutifully, sleepily.

'My hair was coming out in handfuls,' she said, after a pause. She decided not to bother with the rest, which was indeed rapidly fading.

He snorted, secure in his own baldness.

'Is that all? You always were a vain woman.'

Well before six in the evening they were ready to leave. Their plane did not take off till the following morning, but they had decided to avoid an exhaustingly early start then by spending the night at the airport hotel. Long ago, she recalled, they had thought nothing of setting out in the dark after a bare three or four hours sleep, or driving long distances across foreign countries. And that had been in the days when the children were still living with them and needing them. But as you got older your reserves of energy depleted, they had each separately discovered, however brisk and active your outward life.

Now the luggage, the light-weight matching set they had bought the year before with this trip in mind, was outside in the boot of the car. Not their own car – that they had lent to their youngest son. Or supposedly lent. In practice, when they finally got home again, they might let him keep it and get themselves a replacement. They could still afford it, and he was working so hard to get his own company off the ground. Graphic design. A lot of competition in that field, of course. Oh well. He had never (they said to one another) cost them as much as his older brother and sister had, with their long training in medicine and law respectively. And as it happened (though they did not actually say this to each other) he had always been the sweetest-natured of their children.

So the car outside had been lent by a kindly neighbour. They would leave it at the airport, post him the parking ticket, and he would collect at his convenience. All their lives they had been good at making efficient arrangements of this sort with other like-minded people.

'Are we under starter's orders?' said her husband. It was his set phrase for departures, sanctioned by years of use in this context, but produced originally from goodness knows what extinct period of his life or passing relationship: he had never, to her knowledge, been a racing man.

'Yes . . .' she said slowly, preoccupied with a mental review of the contents of her shoulder bag: passports – he had the tickets now – her own traveller's cheques, cash in useful dollar bills (carried separately from the cheques), airsickness pills, short-acting sleeping pills (for jet lag), jersey, spare blouse and change of underwear (in case the

3

main luggage got delayed or even lost), assorted reading matter, tooth-brush, tissues, make-up, her locket with the children's baby hair in it, without which she never travelled any distance . . . She would have unhesitatingly repudiated any suggestion that she was a superstitious woman, yet the locket had become her talisman, a combination of charm and private identity tag.

'Yes,' she said again, with conscious decision. 'Ready, I think. Let's sit down a moment.'

They sat. He – not a superstitious man either, and not a believer in anything if you took him at his own word – counted out loud to three. Then they were officially off.

As he went to the cupboard under the stairs to set the burglar-alarm, she made a hasty retreat out of their own front door. She had never really got used to the alarm, or learnt to treat it nonchalantly as he did. She knew that in practice, once the alarm was set, they had a full half-minute to shut the front door behind them, but she found herself unrealistically scared of cutting her exit fine and risking (horrors!) that before the latch had clicked-to the alarm would start to ring. 'Well, it wouldn't be the end of the world if it did,' her husband would tell her, maddeningly deliberate in his moves, refusing to panic (as he put it). She knew that he was correct. But it was as if, in the depths of her mind, the thirty-second bleeper in the alarm-box was counting out something other, and more significant, than the mere time allowed for shutting the door.

Thus, in a passing flurry of anxiety and urgency, she got herself out of the house – her beloved house, which she would not see again for months – and into the borrowed car. She had thought she would very much mind leaving home this time. Yet, once in the strange car, they seemed to have left already.

The suburban avenue where she knew so many of the occupants by sight or name . . . then the parade of shops along the main road where she was an habitual customer . . . These passed by behind the closed windows of the car like a film which was nothing to do with her. Impossible, now, to envisage stopping, calling in for a packet of biscuits or the evening paper, or even to say 'goodbye'. They had officially departed, and were in an element of their own. They turned their faces to the west. The thickening rush-hour traffic was going the opposite way to them, cars with other people who were caught in the old life, who, at the next dawn, would be asleep in their own beds, not flying off above the clouds into the brightness without frontiers.

In the airport hotel they were in the standard room: she had been in it many times before, accompanying her husband on business trips. In Glasgow, Frankfurt and Milan she had been in it, in New York, Pittsburg, Hong Kong and Tokyo. She knew the bathroom alongside the entrance, with its thick towels, gift-wrapped shower cap and sachets of shampoo, knew the twin beds with the television control panel between them, the twin padded chairs and low table, the large sidelit mirror above what he always claimed was a desk and she maintained was meant as a dressing table. She knew too the soundless, odourless, temperature-less night, with its galaxy of lights below, beyond the double-glazed windows. It was almost like being up in a plane already. Unlike a house, let alone your own house where there were things making silent demands all round you, there was almost nothing to do in that room. At the very most, you might make a phone call, and wash out your tights ready for the next morning, before stretching yourself on the bed with a traveller's paperback. Amazingly restful, not only for the body but also for the mind. Like Eternal Rest. A fragment of the Victorian dream of heaven.

But only a fragment. Because the next day always came. One never had long, not long enough really, to repose in that room. She prepared to luxuriate in the brief time allowed. But her husband seemed restless. He got himself an expensive Scotch from the minibar, then left it standing getting warm under the lamp while he fiddled with his camera. Presently he said abruptly:
'I think I'll just write the odd letter.'

5

'Oh? I thought you'd got all your post done before you left.' He was punctilious about that sort of thing.

He said, in the remote voice of one who does not want to be questioned further:

'I thought I'd just drop a line to each of the children. Sort of – let them know we're off.'

The children. Goodness. He'd hardly ever written to the children. Even when they were away at college – or now, when their eldest son was a doctor at a hospital in the north. He was always happy to chat to them on the phone, but writing had been tacitly regarded as her task. She thought of saying, 'But they know we're leaving tomorrow. We've seen or spoken to all of them in the last three days.' She thought of saying, 'But you haven't anything to tell them yet. Why not wait till we land at Cairo?' Naturally she said neither. He had been on edge these last few days, tense, withdrawn, not like himself really. She opened her book.

What did he usually do in the hotel room at these times? Of course, she realised, on all previous trips within her experience he had had paperwork to do. A file to go through for someone he was due to meet in Frankfurt, Milan or Tokyo. A memo to write up for someone back at home.

But now there were no more files and memos. No more, ever. For the first time, as she lay on the smooth, firm bed under the diffused lights, the reality of her husband's retirement – effectively masked during the unnaturally busy weeks before their departure – came home to her. Something akin to panic stirred within her. What would he do? What would he ever do?

No, she would not think about that now. In any case she had no time to. Weeks – months – out of ordinary time lay ahead of them, a period of repeated departures into the brightness, a succession of arrivals at alien, pristine places, untarnished by experience. No space, in such a life-outside-life, for worry or doubt or long-term dread. All that could wait for the unimaginably distant day of their return. Meanwhile each new stage would be like that lovely hymn – *Morning has broken – like the first morning* . . .

Soothed because it was a hymn, and went back to her

6

childhood, she let the book fall and dozed a little. The past day had, cumulatively, been very tiring, she thought between one absence and another. And she had not slept well the night before. That dream . . . With his back to her, her husband sat and wrote steadily to their children on hotel paper, as if imparting something unprecedented she could not guess or share.

Then, when she woke again, time was no longer spacious but very thin, a mere slice of cold blue light, sharp to the eyes. It was as if it were already compressed by the day ahead which would be no true day, mere hours without weight or character, unnaturally accelerated as they were carried eastwards, into the future.

As the desk clerk handed back the credit card to him, she said to her husband:

'Did you pay the Barclaycard bill up to date?'

'I paid all the bills,' he said, using again that flat, remote voice of one who has temporarily severed contact.

With another small, sudden excess of panic she thought: Oh, I hope he doesn't keep being – like this – while we're away. We'll be together all the time. And if he's – like this – it'll be so lonely . . .

But in the coach going to the terminal he uncharacteristically took her hand a moment and squeezed it.

The terminal at that unreal hour was almost empty, many of the desks still closed. They skirted round one straggling queue of dark-skinned people with copious luggage, and reached their own check-in. There was no one there but the airline clerk.

An experienced traveller, her husband enquired if the bulkhead seats were taken yet and, having secured them, turned back to her triumphantly:

'There, I said we might get those if we turned up in good time. Lots of room for our legs.' To the clerk, he added hopefully: 'Is there a good chance of the third seat that side staying empty? I don't imagine the flight's full, is it?'

'The flight *is* full, Sir, as it happens.'

'Oh – how odd. But I thought . . . Oh well.'

7

The clerk, tapping his computer, made no reply. Their suitcases jolted off down the ramp. As always, she watched them go with a faint pang.

'These are your boarding cards, Sir. Boarding will start in approximately one hour from now. Gate twenty-three.'

'Good. Thank you. We'll go and get some breakfast.'

She was glad that his withdrawn mood had passed. He seemed now almost unnaturally cheerful.

She did not want breakfast. She discovered that she actually felt slightly sick and strange, what she had all her life known as that going-back-to-boarding-school feeling that she tended to get before journeys. She called it that to herself because she had always supposed it was an emotion left over from the unhappiness of youth, long rendered obsolete by the layers of security and happiness that had accrued around her in adult life. But now, as she followed him docilely towards the café, it occurred to her that it did not actually feel like an emotion from the past. No, it was more like a rehearsal for something else. Something long foreseen but still to come.

He had porridge and a croissant and coffee. She had tea. They bought two newspapers and, with abstracted minds, read through British news which already seemed to have become thin and strange like the morning light, artificial approximations to news and daylight rather than the genuine thing.

Later, past Customs and security checks, as they waited on the Departure side amid acres of padded seats, she suddenly said:

'It's not on the monitor.'

'What?'

'Our flight. It ought to be on the monitor by now – it's nearly the time we were told for boarding. But it isn't there.'

He got up himself to study the nearest television screen, fished out the boarding cards to check. She saw him accost a man in uniform, and saw from the man's stance and expression that he was unconcerned by their plight but seemed to be gesturing towards the galleries that led to the departure gates.

With that tightening in her stomach again, she thought wildly: we've miscounted the time, got confused getting up so early – mislaid an hour, even. It must be much later than we thought. Perhaps we've missed the plane . . .

He came back to her, walking deliberately, wearing the aloof expression of one refusing to be made anxious, but he gathered up his own bag quickly.

'He says we'd better get down to Gate twenty-three now. Says the monitors don't always work as they should.'

She was already on her feet, her own bag on her shoulder.

'But there've been no announcements or anything . . . None that we've heard, anyway.'

'Quite.'

They passed rapidly down the galleries, their way speeded by moving belts; they spared hardly a glance at the unrealistic décor of life that still anachronistically and pointlessly continued beyond the toughened glass screens. As if in perfunctory approximation to traditional British weather, a little soundless rain seemed to be falling.

In the Boarding Lounge for Gate twenty-three there was an oddly nondescript collection of people, among whom no particular nationality or race seemed to predominate. Some, like themselves, carried only compact manageable baggage. But some were monstrously laden with super-numary cases and plastic bags, struggling under weights they could hardly lift. Why did the airlines, who theoretic-ally had rules about one piece of hand-luggage only, allow this situation? It wasn't even kind, she thought, to let passengers be so foolish: precious possessions should not become a grievous burden.

With the mixture of amusement and disapproval customary between them at these moments, she drew her husband's attention to their laden companions, adding – 'And lots of them are quite old too, poor things. One wonders why on earth they need to travel with all that stuff?'

Her husband did not answer directly, but said after a moment, in a strained voice:

'There are no children on this flight.'

9

'Well, that's rather a relief,' she said, determinedly bright now that he seemed to have become withdrawn again. 'I mean, it's not that I want to be the sort of person who objects to sitting next to a child on a plane, but when you've spent years bringing up your own children and turning them into reasonable human beings . . .'

He said in the same voice, as if he had not heard her:

'There are not many people here under fifty, for that matter.'

She looked around, and saw what he meant. A silence fell between them. It prolonged itself.

Then they were standing in line. An announcement was now, belatedly, crackling over the loudspeaker; it must – it could only be – their flight being called, but the sound was distorted and people were fussing with luggage and talking all round them; it was impossible to hear properly what was being said.

As they reached the dark-faced official who was collecting parts of the boarding cards she had a strong, helpless desire to say No! – No, there must be some mistake, that this could not be their flight – that it was not time yet, not for a number of years: that anyway she did not want – that her husband wouldn't want – that they hadn't meant –

No use. She could not speak. She saw her husband, at her side, surrender the cards. Too late. They entered the short tunnel that led to the plane.

Heads high, united in a sudden wordless comprehension of which they would now never speak, since there would be no time in which to speak, they entered the aircraft together: a good-looking couple but almost old, suitably equipped for the journey of a lifetime, only lightly laden with the cares of that life, owing nothing; ready, you might say, to go. Or as ready as human beings ever are. At any rate, she thought, in the sudden courage of defeat, they were prepared.

Hardly had they stowed their bags away and seated themselves, than the doors of the plane were closed and the engines revving. The acceleration of time was already taking place.

As they rose into the air, the grass and tarmac and cars and roofs and trees and roads and reservoirs and meadows falling effortlessly away from them forever, that new brightness that she had so long fearfully foreseen, that morning breaking like the first morning, invaded the plane, dazzling her so that she shut her eyes.

Then, for the second time in two days, she opened them on a different realisation. And relief seeped through her.

Prague Fall

'Our roots,' my mother used to say, 'are in Prague.' In English, she used to say it. This phrase, along with 'family tree', give me an image, precise and delicate as in an engraving by Hollar or Dürer, of a gnarled, gothic tree, its roots obtrusively embedded in stones which were pieces of ruined buildings.

My parents still talked German alone together. To us they spoke only English: we grew up essentially ignorant of any other tongue. We had all been born in England: we *were English* we were regularly told, with a fervour and insistence that was itself un-English. It was, however, true. Czechoslovakia, which had nurtured our parents and finally rejected them, causing them to flee for their lives, was to us an intense name, a cipher for something that was over: nothing more. We knew little about the place. But when I became a romantic and self-centred youth, the sort of boy who suddenly looks much too large, this hardly-known country began to figure in my private scheme of things as a land of lost content, a borrowed dream full of castles, bridges with statues, baroque churches, sparkling white snow, trams, 'proper coffee' and feather quilts. I began to complain about England (which my parents, grateful for sheer survival, had always refrained from doing, at any rate in front of us) and to give myself the airs of one born in exile.

My parents' native tongue was German rather than Czech because they both came from that world of assimilated Jewry that was part of Prague before the Second World War. Yet of their Jewish origins they never spoke. That was evidently something that, for them, was buried too deeply to be disturbed. Indeed, it was many years before any of us boys realised that there was any other root down there, twisted round the stones of old Prague, beside our

13

theoretical Czechness. My brothers were never interested in these things anyway.

So when at last I visited the lost land myself, in 1968 when I was twenty-one, it was not to exhume the past but with a vague, heady sense of seeing the future arrive. The Prague spring was in flower, that passing spurt of growth under Dubcek which then went back into hibernation for another two decades. I was in my final year at university. There was much over-optimistic talk of Prague and of the miracle that was unfolding there; and I went to see it in the spring vacation with two friends, delighted with life and with myself for being at the centre of things.

We wandered around the city for a few days, battering off the few contacts we had been able to muster between us, not all of whom turned out to be as conscious of living in a new dawn as we had hoped. (I had no relations left in Prague – for a very obvious reason that did not strike as cold to my heart then, when I was young and careless, as it does today.) It was more by good luck than because of any realistic political involvement that we got to know Kveta and her student friends. It was also the purest good fortune – or so I believed it to be at the time – that she took a particular fancy to me.

Kveta lived in part of a heavy stone house in the Old City, which she and her family thought inconvenient and hard to heat and which I thought the house of my dreams, the exile's true home at last discovered. There was something so un-English about that house; almost, to my eager senses, a whiff of the east. On entering by the street door, you took off your shoes; there were bits of Turkish carpet every-where, even on the chair-backs and tables, and heavy lace edgings to the huge pillows on the hard couch that by night was Kveta's bed. By and by, we began to spend quite a lot of time on that couch, under the ornate, tarnished chandelier. Kveta's father was dead and her mother was out at work all day. Her grandmother was at home, but stayed below in the kitchen pottering over pungent saucepans on the antique gas-stove; anyway, she seemed to like me, in a deaf, smiling way.

14

What else can I say? It was my first love, unique and extraordinary to me but recoverable still only subjectively, as a stab of emotion long healed-over, a small, deep-seated ache somewhere in my mind or body, I am not even sure where. When I try to marshal objective facts about it – to say, 'She was like this – ', or even, 'What we talked about was that – ', I am forced to conclude it was just a first love and no more: anyone's first love. The first primroses and daffodils too were for sale on the street barrows; I used to buy them for Kveta. That is a fact, for what it is worth. I still remember the Czech word for 'flowers' which was not unlike her name, though, to be honest, I cannot entirely recall her face, however much I try. We drank a lot of coffee – proper coffee, of course – and, because we were both still very young, we ate a lot of cakes too. We went for long tram rides. It was my lost land made flesh: which mattered most to me, the place or the person, is not the sort of question you ask yourself at such moments. In the long afterwards, whenever I thought of Kveta, it was always of Kveta-in-Prague, like a little figure in a snowstorm ball, isolated from the rest of life and time.

But life and time were both there. By and by I had to go back to England, to university and my neglected final exams. I'm sure I promised that I would soon return, and I'm sure too that we made plans – why not, in that spring when anything seemed about to become possible? – for her to get a passport and the permission to visit me in England. I say, 'I am sure', but time has consigned any such conversations to oblivion. I merely suppose that we did these things.

At the height of my exams in June I received a letter from Kveta telling me she was pregnant. It was, I suppose, inevitable in the circumstances that I waited a while before sending even a harassed and inadequate reply.

The next thing that happened, as everyone knows, is that the Russian tanks rolled into Prague. The spring, which had seemed to promise so much, was over, and fruitless. Newspapers and magazines were shut down, groups disbanded, relations with foreigners became suspect.

Several people Kveta knew were in jail. There would be no chance now of her being allowed to travel to England, and we both knew it. She did not, in any case, sound as if she wanted to very much any more, if her eventual brief note was anything to go by. I wondered miserably if it had been censured, but I'm afraid that misery was as much for my own sense of guilt as for any real feeling of anguish for her, far away in her snowstorm ball.

So I lost Kveta, and she lost me. So, by saying nothing, doing nothing, I lost any right I might have had over that yet-to-be-born child. The lost land that I had found for those few weeks became lost again to me – doubly lost, for it was now no longer a place of innocent dreams but an Eden from which I had excluded myself by my own behaviour. That probably sounds obsessionally Christian (which I am not) but it is, simply, the way it seemed to me in the end, when it was all irrevocably over.

Of course I did feel very bad about it – as I often told myself during the following winter. I could only say it to myself, since I had told no one else, neither my brothers nor the two friends who had been with me in Prague, what had happened to Kveta. No doubt, by keeping the whole matter to myself, I avoided letting it become entirely real. It was many years and other events later, before I really came to understand that 'what had happened' was my child too. This was certainly stupid of me and callous as well. I can only excuse myself by saying that young men are like that. And (because young men are like that too) by the time the baby was born I was in love with someone else anyway.

I did hear, eventually, that the baby was a girl. The news when it came (in the form of a baptismal announcement on a piece of pasteboard) belonged to someone else's life, not mine. Perhaps, I dimly felt, it belonged to the life I would have led on another loop of time, had my parents not left Prague before my birth and had I not grown up English.

Another twenty-one years passed. Can it be so long? Yes, it must be. I don't seem to have done very much in all that time. My life hasn't been a failure, exactly, I suppose – but I

16

don't feel like talking about that. There would be so much to say. Or else nothing, really, when you come down to it. At least I have a job, though it isn't quite the sort of thing I'd envisaged doing in more ambitious days. And as for Pat . . . No, I don't want to go into all that either. At least Pat and I aren't on too bad terms, now that that's all over as well. I can see the kids every other Sunday (when they're not too busy themselves, that is) which is more than a lot of divorced fathers achieve. But – well, you know how it is: once in a while your past self comes before you, and you cringe and feel glad he can't see you.

In spring 1989 I went back to Prague. The storm of events towards the end of that year were still undreamed of, but there was a lot in the papers about Russian *glasnost* and straws were blowing in the Hungarian wind – I think I probably scented something coming from Czechoslovakia too. I'm still interested in politics, in fact more genuinely interested than I was when I was young, and certainly a hell of a lot more knowledgeable. That's one consolation for not being young any more. Another is coming to realise that, since most of things you do aren't going to make any difference anyway, you might as well be brave – rash, even some people would call it, and pursue your dream if the chance offers. After all, what else is there?

I had this day-dream, you see, about my daughter in Prague. My eldest child. I would look at occasional newspaper pictures of students demonstrating in Wenceslaus Square and imagine that one of those pale smudges was the face of my daughter Sophie. (I knew she had been named Sophie, because it had said so on the baptism card.) I liked to think that, whatever Kveta had or had not made of her life – and a certain passivity and distractability I thought I remembered in her made me suspect that she had not done a lot – my daughter Sophie might now be active in intellectual, dissident circles. Her father's child . . . Well, we all have dreams for our children, don't we? – that they will do better than us along the same lines.

How wonderful it would be if, because of our shared

genes, we took to one another right away! A pristine, exciting relationship, untainted by resentment and learnt scorn: *of course Dad's so hopeless* . . . It did just dawn on me, even in this romantic dream, that Sophie herself might have been brought up to nurse a fairly major resentment against her absent parent, but I gambled on her now being at the stage in life when she would find the idea of me romantic and attractive all the same. The mystery man in her mother's life. The long-lost father returning at last to make amends. Irresistible. Particularly to a Slav soul. Or so I hoped.

I devoted a good deal of thought to how I was actually going to find Sophie. It may sound unkind (well, it is) but I did not much want to meet Kveta again. It was all just too long ago . . . Anyway, an emotion-laden reunion with her was not part of the dream-scenario. It was my daughter I wanted.

However, the only possibility seemed to be an approach to Kveta's old address. I did not want to risk making either her family or myself conspicuous by trying to trace my daughter through more official channels. I tried writing a letter various ways but none of them seemed right. In the end, I just sent a brief note addressed to 'The Occupant' at the house in the Old City, asking if Sophie, the daughter of Kveta Jerni, still lived there, and, if not, whether I might be given her address. I described myself as 'an old family friend', and hoped it wouldn't be Kveta herself who opened it. I wrote it in English but with copies in both German and Czech – supplied by my mother, for whom of course I had to make up some dull story, and who nevertheless asked numerous vague but inquisitive questions. Mother gets bored and lonely these days, on her own. I ought to do more for her really, I know. I do know.

I felt quite exhausted when I'd sent this off, but afterwards told myself that nothing might come of it anyway. The grandmother would be dead; Kveta herself, I realised for the first time, might long since have married respectably, and Sophie might have been brought up under another man's name.

Just once in a long while, however, life does imitate the sentimental artifact of dreams. I had given up really expecting to trace Sophie and was getting interested in quite other plans for my trip to eastern Europe when I received a note from her. Yes, I do mean from Sophie herself. In fractured English too, in a careful schoolgirl's hand.

I do not consider myself a particularly emotional man, but the very sight of that writing, combined with the name on the back of the envelope, made me tremble with feeling.

She said that my letter had been sent on to her and that she was glad to hear from an old friend of her mother's – a remark which might or might not have been meant as a polite way of saying that she knew who I was, and which put me in a fever of speculation. She said that she no longer lived in the Old City but 'on the end of Praha'. She said, almost as an afterthought, or as if she thought I might know anyway, that Kveta was now dead. Had been for some years, it seemed.

That shocked me a bit, of course – she was only my age, why dead so young? – but you see what I mean about life imitating dreams? With poor Kveta gone, a whole great area of potential embarrassment and uncertainty in my approach to Sophie was removed.

She said nothing about her life, her studies, her own dreams, but the very fact that she could write English after a fashion encouraged me to hope, to believe . . . She said that, when I arrived in Prague, she hoped I would come and see her. She said that she was usually at home on Saturdays. Wenceslaus Square, I thought, here I come!

By a piece of substantial good fortune, Prague did not get knocked to bits in the war. The lanes of the old city still curl round the town hall and the main square, and many of the houses in them, including the one Kveta's family used to occupy, have been there for centuries. Beyond the Old City is Wenceslaus Square with its hotels and coffee shops, and a ring of grandiose nineteenth-century buildings. Across the river Kafka's castle keeps watch on everything. I recalled, when I thought hard, other, uglier districts further out: margarine-coloured blocks of flats built by the Soviets in the 1950s and 1960s, but I remembered too that hidden away among these had been old baroque villas, little parks. And the countryside, manifesting itself on the street barrows of the flower-sellers at the first breath of warmth, had never been far off. My daughter now lived on the edge of the city – almost in that countryside, that meant. With some difficulty, I managed to locate the place on my Baedeker map, but the oblongs of green and grey told me little.

For two days, in Prague, I walked round in a concentrated dream, so much coming back to me after twenty-one years that I felt my head would hardly contain it all. On the third day, Saturday, I caught the tram to take me out of the town.

I had always loved the long tram rides Kveta and I used to take, all the way to some terminus where snow-covered hills were close at hand and the air smelt fresh, with whiffs of woodsmoke, and there were beer and sausages for sale in a little shack. Even in the cold we used to have picnics, perched in small groves of birch trees, wrapped together under one rug. I suppose I vaguely imagined (but I can't really say what I imagined, now that that is over too) that I would find my Sophie living in some well-insulated wooden shack set among birch trees, perhaps with a pocket-handkerchief garden at the side meticulously dug and sown with vegetables which now, in May, would be appearing in the good earth. Living like a woodcutter's daughter-cum-lost-princess in a Germanic fairytale.

Clearly I was by this time losing touch with reality. But even if I had had my imagination more firmly in check I would not have been prepared for the place where the tramline finally deposited me. I say 'place', but it was one of those random locations that seem to have parted company with the very notion of place. Everything was filmed with a white-ish powder which, in my disorientation, I took to be dusting of snow even this late in the season. It was a full minute before I realised that it was in fact cement from a works that reared up on the far side of the tramlines and the adjacent railway yards. On the near side, a new-looking

20

motorway and its slip-roads cut the tram terminus off from the nearest human dwellings – a range of towers, white-grey cement themselves, several hundred metres away up a hill.

In muddy corners between road and railways lines there were still a few birches, and even a wooden shack or two, but the cement dust lay on them as well.

After all, hadn't I known that there was a lot of industry round Prague, and that Prague itself was expanding? These were the visible signs of that very prosperity that was now, once again, making Czechslovakians restless. I told myself it would be ignorant and patronising of me to think 'what a pity'. About the cement works, I mean.

Eventually I found the footway that led under the road-complex, and began to walk in the cold, dusty wind toward the distant towers.

I will not go into the details of my false turns, hesitations and vain enquiries once I had got there. Although the development cannot have been standing for many years, it had the run-down, left-about look of a place from which people move on. No one seemed to have heard of Sophie, or to care to help me (which mattered more), or to speak any German; I was even beginning to think of giving up, for that day at least, when I came upon her block-number almost by chance. A grumpy woman with a pushchair, to whom I showed my talisman letter with the precious address, agreed that, yes, this would be the place, but remarked that the only Sophie in the block that she knew of was Mikhael Chotnik's wife on the fifth floor.

'Young?' I insisted, in my feeble few words of what would have been my mother tongue had Hitler not been born.

'*Ja, ja, sehr jung*', the woman agreed contemptuously – and gave me an old-fashioned look before she wheeled her pushchair off, almost as if she suspected me of having romantic designs on Sophie. Which of course I did.

– Or did I? My dream, you may imagine, was now itself battered, windblown and stained with grey dust. What *did* I expect, as I climbed the unregarded staircase, reached the fifth floor and the name 'Chotnik' on a metal plate on a door that children had kicked? A princess in captivity? An intellectual dissident in hiding, forced into the factory, struggling to keep up with her studies at night? Or (as was surely more likely) some juvenile version of the defeated woman downstairs?

I can't tell you. All I can say is, I was not prepared – how could I have been? – for the person who actually opened the door. There on the doorstep, forty years younger, wearing a mini-skirt and a lot of blonde curls but nevertheless entirely recognisable, stood my mother.

When she spoke, in broken English and German, she was someone different: no, not Kveta, just anyone really. But the way she moved, smiled, even the faint gawkiness of the gestures with which she encouraged me into her flat, urged me to sit down on an awful mauve couch – these were unmistakably the traits of the grandmother she had never seen and of whose existence she presumably had no idea.

Or did she? Did she or didn't she guess – know, even – who I was? That, of course, was the question that consumed me, the one I could not ask. Not yet, anyway.

She was self-assured, though, at any rate on the surface. That was the first thing I registered. I had vaguely envisaged – hoped? – that I would be the one to set my shy, wondering daughter at ease. But the boot was very much on the other foot.

She offered tea in a glass, sugary biscuits, whisked back and forth from the kitchen in her ridiculous skirt, contained and finally shut in the bedroom a clamorous dog, answered the telephone with a stream of effusive Czech which I somehow felt was directed at me, beached on the sofa, rather than at the person on the other end of the line. Finally she plonked herself opposite me with a saleswoman's smile and said what a great pleasure it was to receive an old friend of her dear Mama. Her Mama, who God had taken in a train crash two years before – but perhaps I knew that? – had no doubt often spoken of me. Yes, she, Sophie, was sure poor Mama had spoken of me.

'?'

Yes, yes, poor Mama (who had had rather a hard life, I no

22

doubt understood) had often spoken of the friends of her youth and what a nice time they had all had.

I said (really there was no other possible thing to say) that I too had the fondest memories of Kveta. Plunging round in the soggy cavern of my memory for something else to add, I came upon Kveta's pale, slightly ethereal good looks and upon stray recollections of her discoursing on Kafka and Rilke to my respectfully ignorant attention. I intimated to her daughter that when I had known Kveta she had been a serious student and politically aware: had she perhaps gone on to teach – or to a career in journalism, or – ?

My mother sitting opposite me shook her head and laughed her slightly hectic, dismissing laugh. Oh no! No. Mama – Kveta – had always worked hard for her living. (In this single phrase I felt Sophie dispose so implacably of the liberal professions that I did not dare to mention them again.) In the years before her sudden death she had worked in the large department store on Republiky – Kotva – perhaps I knew it? It was a new building. In the china and glass department – like this! She tapped the tea-glass she was holding, on which a painted mannequin presented a bunch of flowers to a little girl who seemed to be without her knickers. She, Sophie, currently worked there too. Kotva was quite a nice place and already she was at the top grade possible for her age; she had been there since leaving school five years before. However, she was planning to leave soon because a new shopping centre was due to open out here. Very modern, for the new housing estates. It would be more convenient to work near home.

I wanted to say, 'But then you will miss the heart-lifting experience of going into the real Prague each day. Your life then will be nothing but these towers, the cement works, a garish shopping mall, this despoiled land that is neither country or town.' I wanted to say, 'Sophie, your mother was really quite an ordinary girl who had acquired an intellec-tual veneer by associating with brighter students – but she had some general idea of beauty and culture and style, at any rate when I knew her: did she pass nothing of this on to you? Did unsupported motherhood – my perfidy – or just

23

life itself destroy all that in her? Or what? Or have *you* turned your back on culture for reasons of your own? You are bright, or you would not speak so much English. What happened in all those years of your growing up, the years I should have watched over and did not?'

Of course I did not ask. For one thing, I was painfully conscious the entire time that I had long ago abdicated from the right to question or criticise. And for another thing, it is difficult to ask questions about a negative fact. Had Sophie (who was prattling on now with focussed assurance about the price of this and that) shown the faintest sign of interest in the way her country was governed, I would have taken up the subject eagerly. But when someone is chatting about the availability of spare parts for a Lada you cannot suddenly say, 'Why are we talking about this rather than about the probable effects of *glasnost* on the press or the banned satirical plays of Vaclav Havel?' Or at any rate *I* can't.

At another level, I was afraid, I think. Afraid that she really did know who I was, for all her bright politeness, and that the remarks about Kveta's hard life were a code warning me to keep my distance. Perhaps I was imagining things – her faintly aggressive air was probably habitual to her, and not provoked by me. But it was hard not to imagine things when she sat there laughing and talking like my own mother in travesty. It was as if we were both acting assumed roles. And yet, on reflection, I don't believe that she was. As for me – well, it seemed after all that I had no real role to play.

I had intended to tell her who I was. Yes, I really had intended to, even after she had opened the door, even after the tea was produced. But I found now, after everything, that I wasn't going to.

It was therefore a relief rather than otherwise when her husband appeared. Her husband – yes, of course, she was married already, at twenty-one (the age I had been at her conception), she with her mauve couch and her awful tea-glasses and her pictures of birches at sunset, and her great squishy double bed that I had glimpsed through the bedroom door when the dog was shut away. She hadn't

24

mentioned that she was married, I think, but no doubt she had assumed the fact was obvious.

Husband was dark, muscular, a faintly ingratiating type quite a few years older than she was. He worked in the cement factory and was in his dust-laden overalls. He did not appear to speak any English, and very little German, but before he went off to have a bath he tried to get me to change some money with him as if a foreigner was a species he knew only from street observation and which existed only for this particular purpose. Dollars? he suggested hopefully, but with a hint of genial brutality also – Deutschmarks? No? Well – Hungarian Forints then? Surely I had *something* other than Czech Kroner? He would give me a good rate, I need not worry. Honest Joe, that was him.

Sophie, to do her justice, looked a little embarrassed, and shut him up with a stream of placatory Czech. He went off noisily to have his bath, and I left before he could return.

I had meant to say, 'I'll look you up again,' – a meaningless phrase, perhaps, but one leaving open a little crack for fate or chance or a change of heart. But at the last moment I could not say it.

Sophie thanked me effusively but rather quickly for my visit, and had shut the door of the flat before I was down the first flight of stairs.

As I walked through that estate, where other men were now returning from work, other alien women pursuing their lives, I thought: I shall never know now if she knew. That was my chance. And it's gone.

I do tend to talk to myself like that. A silly habit, no doubt. This time, even as I formed the words, I knew they were empty. There had never been any chance at all. Sophie was not my daughter in any sense that could hold meaning for either of us. The door to that particular lost land had been shut before she was born. A failure is a failure. And even God, it is said, cannot alter the past. Even supposing that He wanted to. Since I have never noticed much evidence of good judgement on His part, perhaps He was quite satisfied with the way things were. Stupid old man.

The day before I left Prague to move on to other, peacefully virgin territories such as Vienna and Budapest, I visited the Old Jewish Cemetery. I can't think how it was that I never found my way there before, long ago. I suppose I was just not interested enough, in those days, to seek it out in its inconspicuous corner near the river behind its high wall. I suppose that Kveta, whom I seem now to remember being vaguely anti-Semitic in an unthinking, Slav way, never mentioned it to me. Well, I never mentioned to her that I was Jewish, and she was probably too innocent to notice.

Most cemeteries suggest the sunken repose of death and the irretrievable past. Here, I found when I got in, the dead were alive. The stones were so thickly packed together, and stuck out of the ground at such wild angles, that it seemed as if the people they represented must be in permanent movement below, heaving and pushing, quarrelling, embracing, praying. And the stones themselves, fretted all over with that square lettering I shall never learn to read, were cream and beige and reddish brown, the colours of bone and flesh that have become petrified soil themselves: Jewish earth!

Here, if anywhere, I thought, our family roots lie, down below the levels of modern Prague and Victorian Prague and even below Renaissance Prague, down in the medieval world of the ghetto and the alchemists, of the persecuted and the obscure, of the thinkers and visionaries. Kafka's ancestors and my ancestors and those of the intellectual élite of modern America besides. A land without frontiers, nothing to do with Czech nationalism or anti-Communist demonstrations in Wenceslaus Square; a cultural heritage that even God cannot destroy. Who needs posterity when he has such a past? Not me.

Shanti and the Oranges

Shanti had worked herself into such a state of elation about her marriage and her journey to what, in Bengal, they called *Yookay*, that it was a full two years before her naturally buoyant and optimistic spirits had floated right down again. And even then it was many months before she faced the shaming, secret fact that she was not as entirely happy as she had expected to be – that, in fact, she was not really happy at all.

'Just now', Shanti said to herself in the careful English she still made efforts to study and improve, 'I am not being too happy. I have some problems,' she added aloud, more confidently, pleased with the sound of the phrase. But there was no one to hear it: the quiet, tidy room remained unmoved by her revelation. The clock went on ticking, the landlord's shabby brown leatherette settee went on sitting smugly in its place before the unlit electric fire, and Shanti's brass ornaments on the shelf above went on reflecting her fluffy orange rug and so creating an illusory impression of warmth in the chilly air. Today the falseness of this struck Shanti: pretended heat – like the pretended happiness she had been trying to sustain all these months.

She had been so proud of that rug, those ornaments, when she was newly married. Now, suddenly overcome by the awareness of her present difference from that eager girl, she turned her head away. Tears stung her eyes and she dabbed at them with the end of her sari, at first angrily then, calming, with more care. If she messed her eyes she would have to do them all over again before Anil came home. She had no objection to spending time at that – she had plenty of time – but she was worried about using up her dwindling supplies of make-up too quickly and having to ask . . . He would give her a little money, of course, but . . .

She ran to the fireplace and perched unsteadily on the

27

kerb to look into the gilt-framed mirror above, which was hung just a little too high for someone of Shanti's size. Good: the black was not smudged, or nothing that she couldn't repair with the corner of a hanky. She did so, very carefully, then took another long look at her smooth face, her desirably light brown skin, her lovely mouth, her little gilt earrings that tinkled when she walked. However changed she might feel in her spirit, the girl who looked back at her was, in appearance, exactly the same one who had married Anil. Today, the mark at the centre of her forehead was green, to match her green sari. Tomorrow, it might be light red, or reddish brown, or even blue. Deciding each morning what her colour scheme would be for that day was something to which Shanti looked forward. Though once or twice recently, on days when Anil was not coming back till late, or was away on business altogether, she had caught herself wondering rather desperately what or whom she was making herself beautiful *for*?

Somehow, it was not a question you would ever ask yourself, at home in Bengal, where there were people day and night to admire you, love you, admonish you, talk to you and even argue or quarrel with you if that was the way you or they felt. The bungalow where Shanti had been brought up, built by her grandfather and now owned by her oldest uncle, was full of people – aunts, cousins, sisters, a brother and his wife. But even if Shanti had not had the good fortune to belong to a large, prosperous and self-respecting family she knew she would never have been alone, not in Dacca, not like she was here, in London NW20. In Dacca, in Calcutta and any other town she had visited, there were always people. People walking in the streets or selling things or carrying on their trades or begging or just standing about watching other people. Yet here, it seemed, there was no one – or almost no one.

There was Anil, of course, and she felt guilty about these feelings when she thought of him, for he was a considerate, responsible husband, a hard worker and a good business-man, just as her uncles had promised her he would be when the match was arranged. But Shanti had never expected to

28

rely entirely on him for company as well – she had simply never contemplated such a possibility. Anyway, most of the time he wasn't there.

Shanti wandered back to the window to see if, this time, there was anyone passing on the pavement outside – anyone at all. But it wasn't the sort of pavement where people passed much, at least not on foot.

The house where Shanti and Anil rented their two-room first-floor flat was in a short row of gabled, semi-detached ones, set back on their own bit of pavement with a strip of muddy grass between them and the main road, which was the North Circular. On the North Circular, the traffic was non-stop, which Shanti construed logically as meaning that individual cars never stopped. It was, she thought sadly, a road for people going somewhere else. In their eyes her home wasn't a place, it was a non-place, she reflected.

To think she had been so proud of the address when she had printed it out for her parents in her first letter to them! *North Circular Road* had sounded so grand, and she had been enormously impressed, also, by the cleanness and spaciousness and quietness of it all. True, the main road itself was a little noisy, but their run of houses and the other streets behind, with their fresh paint and neat gardens and absence of anyone squatting on the corners, seemed to her amazingly exclusive. She had concluded delightedly that only the rich lived here, and that her brother and uncles had, if anything, underestimated the case when they had told her that Anil's Import-Export business was doing well and that he had excellent prospects.

It had taken her, she thought soberly, till quite recently to realise that the status of people like Anil, far from being higher here than in Dacca, was actually lower. Millions of people around London lived in houses like this one, literally millions: it meant nothing, no one respected you for it particularly, though Anil himself hardly seemed to realise it.

But long before this painful truth had been born in on her, while she still took pleasure in arranging the two rooms tastefully and having everything nice for her husband,

29

Shanti had already been puzzled by the district in which she found herself. Gradually, as she had got bolder, she had ventured out alone on little walks. The residential roads at the back of their house twisted and turned without leading anywhere in particular, and she became afraid of getting lost there. She tried, instead, going one way along the big road, though it was not pleasant walking there with so many lorries and cars passing. But she only came to a kind of wasteland, with railway lines and smoking tips and an electricity station and a canal and patches of uneven mud and grass for all the world like the outskirts of Calcutta, except that in such an area of Calcutta there would have been people living there too – *bustee*-dwellers hanging on to their squalid shanties, busy and intent. Here there was no one, except some men working behind the Electricity Board fence, who whistled at her.

Horrified, she had turned for home and had never gone back that way, though she and Anil regularly passed it on their fortnightly trips to see an Indian film in Southall, all the way round the North Circular. Shanti loved these evenings out; they were the high points of her existence, and to sit in the car and then in the dark of the cinema and then in the car coming home again she always wore her most beautiful saris.

She longed to go to the cinema more often: every week, rather than every other week, would have been wonderful. But Anil was so busy, it was kind of him to make time to take her out as it was – and anyway they were trying to save all the money they could for the house of their own Anil wanted to buy. That was why she lived as economically as she could, wrapping herself in a shawl during the day rather than switching on the fire, making her boxes of face and eye-paint last, never asking for money for herself if she could help it.

He never refused her outright, but he would insist on knowing exactly what she wanted it for, and it was hard to explain; she could not save anything out of the expense-money he gave her daily, for that was only small sums for their immediate needs – for milk, and a few fresh vegetables

30

and occasionally a little meat. The rest of their food Anil bought himself from a big discount store near his work and brought home in the car, which of course was very thoughtful of him: large bags of lentils and split peas and flour, oil and *ghee* in outsize cans, spices in containers marked *For the Catering Trade Only*.

At first she had not done any of the shopping, but then, walking the other way along the main road, she had discovered a small run of shops and had persuaded Anil to let her buy certain things there. It had cheered her up when she had discovered the Parade (that was what it was called): it seemed almost like a place. There was a butcher, a small Express Dairy and a chemist and a baker selling the tasteless, odourless cakes British people liked to eat, and two newspaper and sweet shops and a shop that sold paint and wallpaper and two more that were always changing hands and presently stood empty.

Shanti liked the elderly chemist best. He would talk to her sometimes about the weather, and one cold day he asked her, 'Don't you feel it, coming from where you do?' She had just smiled at him and said, 'It isn't too bad.' Afterwards she wished she had said something more interesting which would have made him want to go on talking to her, but she had not had much practice at that. It wasn't just because there were people there that she liked the Parade: the house fronts above the shops were covered uniformly in white tiles, with a decorative green motif running all the way across the top, and Shanti thought it was beautiful.

She would miss the Parade when they did buy their own house. Anil was so keen on the idea, but she was coming to realise with dread that it might well turn out to be in a place still more nondescript than their present home. She had been driven around the northern suburbs of London just enough to have some awareness of that pinky-grey universe stretching as far as the mind can imagine and further, neat house after neat house, dull road after dull road, confusing mile after mile . . . At times, her heart shrank at the thought. At others, she comforted herself by dreaming that they might move to a road with other Bengalis in it, that she might even find a friend to go out with.

She wished they could have moved to Southall, where there were proper Indian shops and all those cinemas and you could buy Bengali newspapers, but when she had plucked up the courage to ask Anil if they could look for their house in Southall he had made the slight face of someone passing a particularly dirty beggar or smelling a bad smell. She had understood then that Southall wasn't good enough for him. He wanted somewhere more English, more refined. There were, he explained gently, some rough, low-class people in Southall.

Because of never having any money of her own, Shanti could not go very far. In any case, even had she had the money for a bus, she would have been afraid of getting on one of those that passed her house in case it should carry her too swiftly off into unknown regions from which she could never find her way back. It was therefore more than eighteen months before she discovered the Brent Cross Shopping Centre.

It was quite a walk there, but it was worth it, once she knew about it. Oh my goodness, yes. Since that discovery most of Shanti's isolated moments of happiness had been passed at Brent Cross.

Shanti did not know that the huge complex, set against the flying landscape of an urban motorway intersection, was modelled on an American prototype and had provoked much controversy in the building. All she knew was that, once inside its swing doors, it was like being transported into another world – a beautiful place of colour and warmth and wonderful objects and happily moving crowds. There was a central arcade and flowers in tubs and even a fountain, with people sitting round it. There was invisible music. It was just like a lovely, huge, covered bazaar, only without the noise and dirt you usually found in a bazaar, and without anybody pestering you. You could wander round there all day if you liked, looking at things, and no one would mind. In fact Shanti sometimes did.

She did not tell Anil about Brent Cross. She suspected

32

that he knew about it already, but, if so, his reason for not mentioning it to her could only be that he didn't particularly want her to go there. It would be too awful if she were to tell him about it only to have him forbid her to go there. At twenty, two years married, Shanti was learning guile. She longed to write to her mother and sisters about this wonderful place, particularly as her letters to them these days tended to be rather short on wonderful things, but there again silence seemed more prudent. She was sure that her letters were read out in the household, and just suppose one of her uncles should write something back about her and Brent Cross in a business letter to Anil. No, she must keep it to herself.

The year before, she had learnt a sobering lesson about Anil. When he had come to Dacca for their marriage and she had met him for the first time, he had seemed, in contrast to some of the people she knew, so modern-minded and Western that her sisters and cousins had envied her. 'You are lucky, Shanti,' her eldest sister had said ruefully. 'That one will treat his wife with respect – just like a real British man.' Yet although this was true, and although Anil was indeed thoughtful and gentle, Shanti had come gradually to understand that his ideas on a wife's place and on her necessary obedience differed hardly at all from the ideas of her oldest uncles.

She had vaguely hoped – it seemed silly now – that in coming to live in Britain she would somehow benefit from all the things British women benefitted from. Shanti had read magazines which reprinted stories with Western backgrounds: she knew that British and American women had jobs and careers, even when they were married. Shanti had never particularly wanted a career (one of her cousins, not married, and plain, was a teacher: everyone said how devoted she was to *her* children, and such a high-minded alternative to matrimony was not at all to Shanti's taste). But a small job, now, was another matter. It would be so lovely to have people to talk to and something to do! Say, for three or four hours every day when Anil was safely at business and didn't need her. And it would be lovely too to earn some money for her own expenses.

33

So when the chemist in The Parade advertised for a part-time assistant behind the counter, she plucked up her courage to mention it to Anil, hinting that perhaps she herself might take it just for a few months, till they moved to their own house. . . ? And the money she might earn would be useful, wouldn't it? But he turned her suggestion down instantly with one of his looks of well-bred disgust.

Timidly, knowing already that it was useless and that it had been ridiculous of her to dream such a dream, she tried to excuse herself:

'But it is a nice place, Anil, they are nice, refined people . . .'

'*They*, perhaps, but what about the customers? And a chemist's shop sells all sort of things, not all of them very . . . Do you think I want *my wife* selling objects and remedies to sick strangers? Why, you might catch something.'

The stress he laid on the words *my wife* had always made her proud before. Now, momentarily, she found herself almost hating him and his smug, invariable assumptions about her and about life. She hated the way he tucked his chin in, crumpling his mouth primly when he disapproved of something. And she hated the luxuriant way in which he sometimes sniffed.

It was because she was so upset at discovering such emotions within herself that she made a big scene that night, for the first and only time, sobbing and crying herself into a state till Anil became genuinely concerned. It was then that he said:

'You will feel quite different about this, Shanti, once we have children.' And she had seized on this, as perhaps he had hoped she would as a pretext and an excuse for everything.

It was true (of course) that she hoped for children, and true that as yet there was no sign of any. Perhaps it *was* the case, as Anil was now gently urging, that once there was a baby in prospect she would feel differently about everything. It was in any case easier and pleasanter to believe that a baby was the only thing missing in her life than it was to

34

pursue her secret forebodings to a more alarming conclusion. When Anil suggested that perhaps he should take her to a doctor to find out why she was not yet pregnant, she wept tears of genuine love and gratitude.

The doctor was an Indian; not a Bengali, but he spoke in Hindi to them and she liked him very much. In fact she felt so relieved and comforted by his cheerful, matter-of-fact manner that it was almost as if the problem had been solved by this one visit. But it turned out that this doctor could not do much himself beyond advising her to take her temperature every morning and not to worry. Instead, he sent her to a specialist, a lady doctor in a big hospital a long way across the miles of London.

Shanti was glad it was a lady (Anil seemed relieved about that too) but she did not actually like this new doctor half as much as the other one: she talked too fast for Shanti to understand properly and always seemed in a hurry. It was also a great pity the hospital was so far away, as each time Shanti had an appointment Anil had to take time away from his work to take her there. He was very kind about it and did not complain, but as they were shunted about to wait on chairs she could feel his relentless, controlled impatience, and that made her more nervous and miserable than the doctor's probing instruments.

She had various tests and some pills to take for a few months. Then the doctor said she should have something called a 'post coital test'. She explained it to them together. It was to check that Anil's seed was strong enough, she said: often the 'fault' turned out to be with the husband.

Shanti felt herself going hot and cold with embarrassment for Anil as the doctor's flat, graceless voice rose and fell, and when they came out of the consulting room together she dared not look at him. Neither on the way home nor later did they discuss what the doctor had said.

Shortly after that, when Anil was going away on a business trip to Manchester, he rented a television set as a surprise for Shanti. She was so touched and delighted that she actually cried again. The television did help fill the limitless space left by Anil's absence and Shanti's English

35

quickly improved on a diet of daytime programmes for children. But when she screwed up her courage on Anil's return to whisper to him that she was so glad he was home tonight because the next day she had her appointment for that test, his face closed.

'A man cannot be ordered about in these matters, Shanti,' he said stiffly. And that night he did not come to bed till after she had at last fallen wretchedly asleep.

He would not cooperate; and she knew that he was not a person who changed his mind about things. For weeks she wondered obsessively if she could possibly devise a way of going behind his back . . . Make a secret appointment at the hospital – but how. . . ? She had no money and no idea of the way, and in any case she quailed at the enormity of the deception involved. And suppose she did, by some means or other, manage it all? And suppose the lady doctor just said, 'Yes, the problem is with your husband. He must come back and see me himself.' Where would that get her?

The morning when she stood in her green sari looking out on the passing cars was only one of a seemingly endless succession of mornings and afternoons, when she had occupied herself turning the weary problem round and round in her mind so much that by evening it almost seemed disintegrated, as an object ceaselessly fumbled in the hands loses shape and texture. Yet every morning it was there again like a hard, round ball of some irreducible matter. The morning she wore the green sari was only different from all the others because that was the one on which she at last made up her mind to go on her own to see the first doctor, the cheerful Hindi-speaker.

She had got directions to this surgery from the elderly chemist in the Parade, with whom she had continued a subdued friendship over the purchase of her pills. She guessed that he must know what she was taking them for, and sensed that he felt sorry for her.

To her horror – what *was* the matter with her? – she found herself bursting into tears once more in the doctor's office. He was very nice about it, and gave her fistfuls of paper handkerchiefs and told her once again not to worry:

36

lots of husbands were like Anil, he said, even those who dearly wanted sons. It was a pity, but that was the way it was. He advised her to go on taking her pills anyway, and gave her a prescription for tranquillisers as well. 'You're very young still,' he said. 'You've got a lot of time ahead of you.' He meant, she realised afterwards, 'You've plenty of time yet to have your children,' but she at first interpreted it otherwise, suddenly seeing in horrible clarity the years ahead before her like a desolate grey vista: a line of dull houses with shut windows, an empty pavement, beyond it a wet, wide road with monotonously sighing traffic, and over everything a dank, chilly drizzle, muddying and darkening everything it touched. She cried then in real horror – oh, not for a child: secretly, she had never been that keen on a child anyway – but she cried for herself and her life. *Her life.*

The doctor seemed harassed. He patted her shoulder and told her to sit quietly in the waiting room till she felt better. She sat there till the last patient had left. 'We're closing now, dear,' said the receptionist. She hesitated: 'Don't you want to go home and have your dinner?'

Dinner was the last thing Shanti wanted, and anyway recently she hadn't bothered with anything much to eat till Anil came home at night, but she had been brought up to be polite. 'Thank you,' she said. 'Yes, I'll go home to dinner now.'

She went instead to the chemist and had her prescription for tranquillisers made up. Then, greatly daring, she asked the chemist's wife, who was behind the counter, for a glass of water to take two right away. The lady supplied the water, but she and her husband dubiously watched Shanti as she swallowed.

'I should go home now, if I were you, dear. You look ever so tired. Have a little sleep before your husband comes home.'

'Yes,' said Shanti politely. 'Yes, I think I will do that.' Why did everyone keep urging her to go home? She spent quite enough of her days there as it was.

Once back on the North Circular she turned the opposite way from her home. It was a cold, lowering day, and an intermittent wind blew grit against her face so that she covered it with the end of her sari. It wasn't at all a nice day for a forty minutes' walk to Brent Cross, but she didn't care, she was going there.

She had no particular purpose when she entered the place; she just wanted, as each time before, to forget herself there, to wander suspended in light and warmth, to gaze at intricate things, to finger soft stuffs and plan what she would buy if she were rich. She had by now her favourite places in the Centre, shops she visited ritualistically, savouring them each in turn.

There was the carpet department, and the curtain department near it full of figured damask that Shanti greatly admired. There was a shop that had lovely silk scarves and beads and another that sold table lamps whose stands held rythmically winking, swimming globules of oil: she longed for one of those lamps, but it was impossible, they cost pounds and pounds. She longed still more for a life-sized china dalmation dog, who stood in a ground floor shop flanked by great pots of ferns and screens that she recognised as Indian work, but of course the dog was unthinkably expensive, and anyway where would she put it? She patted its cool china head, in the way she had seen people pat real dogs, and it seemed to be looking at her. She whispered to it in Bengali . . .

It was then that she caught sight of the oranges. They were all together in a Benares brass bowl and at first glance she had taken them for real, but of course they weren't real, like the dog, that was the point of them. They were exactly like real oranges in every particular, except that they were made of hard, shining porcelain. They were a lovely colour.

She went closer to look. By and by she touched one. It was cool, as the dog had been. She stepped back to admire them all in the bowl that reflected and enhanced them, and then realised what they reminded her of: her brass ornaments at home. If only, *only* she had one eternal orange like these to put among them.

She was used to yearning for things. It was not until she felt her heart beating and her throat dry that she realised,

38

with an odd abstraction, that this time – this time – she was going to do something about it.

She glanced quickly round the department. There were never many people in there; it wasn't like the dress shops along the arcade with their throngs of absorbed, critical women. This afternoon the only person anywhere near was a gawky woman in trousers and an anorak who was dreamily contemplating some quartz chess sets.

Shanti carefully loosened the end of her sari, which she had tucked into her waistband, and re-draped it round her head and her breast. In its all-inclusive folds, no bulge would be visible. Then she stretched out a quick hand and took first one orange and then, on second thoughts, another to go with it.

She had them securely wrapped in the gauzy folds with her hand supporting them. She was walking with dignity and assurance in the direction of the main exit doors when another hand, much heavier than her own, descended on her arm and gripped it. Shanti jumped violently, but clutched her oranges to her. Someone towered over her: it was the woman in trousers and anorak. She didn't look gawky or dreamy now. She looked threatening and very sure of herself.

'I am a store detective and I must ask you to accompany me to the manager's office. Do you understand?'

For one wild moment Shanti thought it was the lady doctor from the hospital, sent to arrest her for failing to come for her test. The accent and manner seemed the same, flat and offhand yet tense at the same time. She wanted to cry, 'Oh Anil, you were right, she's bad, save me!' but then like a second wave another thought broke across the first: Anil was in league with this woman – Anil had sent her to spy, and would soon be here himself to confront Shanti with her failure, as a wife and a person. Anil had known about her deceitful visits here all the time. He would despise and reject her now, and then she would be neither wife, girl nor widow, a non-person in a non-place, her life over before it had even begun. Nothing lay before her but Anil and death, death and Anil, death and annihilation.

She opened her mouth then and began to scream, and a crowd of people began to gather round her.

Victory

Mary Spencer-Byrd had been elected on to the Cemetery
Committee for the same reason that she was elected on to a
number of local committees: she was an energetic single
woman of advancing years with no job, no apparent
disabilities and no evident worries. She was also – though
most of her fellow committee members would have
refrained from stating the fact baldly in these democratic
days – a member by birth of the class which has traditionally
provided people to sit on parish councils and Benches, to
run civic societies and conservation groups and fund-
raising campaigns, to impede the opening of new motor-
ways and to prevent the closure of old footpaths, and in
general to referee the creaking and complex machinery of
English society over its own particular territory.

Mary's territory was the old village of Woodgate some
nine miles from central London, around which have grown
since the First World War the great suburbs of Woodgate
East, Woodstow and Hayling. Mary could remember when
Woodgate village green, which was now smoothly mown
and protected by white posts and chains and flower-beds,
had had sheep grazing on it. She could remember when
there were open fields between Woodgate and the Underground line at Hayling: the Tube had stopped there in those
days. She could remember when Mr Lucas had done his
own butchering in the yard behind his bloody, fly-infested
shop in the narrowly picturesque High Street: today the
street's picturesqueness had been carefully preserved,
though marred by the traffic that every day almost clogged
it, but 'Mr Lucas's' (as she still called it in her mind) sold
cotton clothes in Provençal prints, hand-made jewellery,
and cloth bags encrusted with peasant embroidery done in
factories near Bombay.

She could also remember when all the white stuccoed

41

houses round the green, and all the big red-brick ones down Chestnut Avenue and the Grove that were now occupied by bankers or lawyers or well-known actors, or divided into flats, had belonged to old Woodgate families, including her own. But she did not often refer to those times, for she had long ago determined that no one should ever class her as a silly old dear yearning for a past that would never return. In any case, some of these new people (she still secretly thought of them as 'new', the families who had moved there in her own youth as London expanded between the wars) were quite splendid: well-educated, public-spirited, most capable and influential. Woodgate had certainly been fortunate, for without them to keep an eye on things the state of the village today might have been very different. Whenever Mary drove down to Hayling to Marks & Spencer's or Sainsbury's, or over through Woodstow and the new housing estates there on the way to see her sister in Buckinghamshire, she shuddered inwardly to think of the tide of uncaring, wanton change that might so easily have swamped Woodgate itself had she and all the other concerned people been less vigilant all these years . . .

Why, without their presence the Cemetery Committee would never have been set up. What would have happened to the wonderful old place, all twenty-one acres of elaborate sculptury set now, for the most part, in dense undergrowth, if the residents of Woodgate Village had not been on the alert in the 1960s when the Cemetery Company had finally decomposed into liquidation? – as the chairman of the Committee had so amusingly put it. Apparently a cemetery that was too full for any new graves did not represent an asset but, rather, a formidable liability: maintenance costs had risen and risen and the sums of money that families like the Spencer-Byrds had covenanted long ago to have their family plots cared for 'in perpetuity' had been rendered derisory through time and inflation. Funny to think that once, besides being one of the most fashionable places in the London area for burial, the place had also been a 'very sound investment'. Mary's own grandfather had had shares in it, and he had been an astute investor, as Mary's own continuing private income, even in these difficult times, testified. She sometimes contemplated with a kind of placid wonder the fact that her present modest comfort derived from fatherly and grandfatherly foresight from over a hundred years ago. Good things *could* last, given care and watchfulness . . . A heritage . . . For the benefit of future generations . . . (And similar phrases.)

That was what the cemetery was also. And goodness knows what horrors of municipal good intentions the local borough council would have perpetrated when the cemetery came under their reluctant charge had it not been for herself and the rest of the Committee stepping into the breech! In the course of many years' sterling work on committees (always 'sterling' in votes of thanks) Mary had imbibed a patchy legal knowledge, and she was aware that no powers, short of a special Act of Parliament, could have enabled the council to use the place for a new housing development, as the more vociferous and brutish councillors had apparently hoped. But their planning department could have wrought its own subtle desecration: wholesale stone removal . . . cement paths . . . municipal daffodils . . . a children's playground, forever being vandalised . . . Disliking children, she shuddered inwardly; she had been a spectator for many decades of the doctrinaire crassness of local councils. She had sometimes wondered if she ought to have stood for the council herself when she was a little younger, to help combat their stupidity at close quarters, but she felt (as she told her friends) that she really could not have *endured* the company of some of those people from Hayling and East Woodgate . . . The present Committee, of course, was a very different affair, being largely composed of Woodgate Village people with only a few docile outsiders to represent other interests.

They were talking, this evening, about the Dinshaw-Thacker grave: Item 5 on the agenda. In fact it seemed to have been an item on the agenda at every meeting for at least a year, and although they had had much encouraging discussion nothing had actually been decided. J. G.

43

Dinshaw-Thacker, the famous Indian cricketer, had died of pneumonia in 1909 on his first and only visit to London, and had been buried by a sorrowing multitude in the cemetery whose comprehensively non-denominational nature was well known. The secretary was of the opinion that the M.C.C., with whom he said he was in 'close correspondence', might be persuaded to come up with a few hundred to restore the monument – a giant marble wicket, bowled by an enormous ball. But Mr Rammage the treasurer, who tended to cast himself in the role of hard-headed businessman and shatterer of illusions, scoffed at this: the M.C.C. wouldn't waste their funds on the memory of a foreigner, he said, however illustrious; Dinshaw-Thacker's own lot should be persuaded to divvy up. After all, there was no shortage of them these days. Hayling was full of 'em.

The chairman, with a slightly anxious glance at Mr Rammage, who did tend to get going rather, said that this was certainly an idea. Perhaps one of them should approach the leader of the London Hindu community, whomsoever that might be?

'But Dinshaw-Thacker was a Parsee,' said Mr Tobin, a rather colourless architect who, however, occasionally knew things. Mary wondered fleetingly if he had been born in India. She glanced at his finger-nails.

'Does that make a difference?'

'If he'd been a Hindu he wouldn't have been buried anyway. Hindus burn their dead. Actually Parsees are supposed to put their dead in roofless towers to be pecked to bits by vultures – towers of silence, they're called. But I suppose there weren't any of those in London . . . Probably still aren't.'

'And not many vultures,' said a woman member of the Committee with a nervous giggle.

Rammage snorted. 'Disgusting. I should think not. How they can, beats me.'

But is it disgusting? thought Mary. Is it really any more disgusting than putting someone to rot in a varnished box underground? And how can people do that, when they really think – *really* think – what it means? Most people have no imagination, and just as well.

Her mind slid back on an accustomed track to her own family grave, not very far from Dinshaw-Thacker's as it happened, on the western side of the cemetery. Her grandparents were there, and her parents, but for some reason she never contemplated their continuing presence in that place, perhaps partly on account of a vestigial childhood belief that they were 'really' in heaven. The only person she felt to be in the grave was her brother Nigel. When her skimming imagination stripped away the layers – the cow parsley and nettles first, then the stone, then the earth, then the varnished lid – it was Nigel who lay revealed to her.

She had never mentioned to anyone on the Committee that she had this personal stake in the cemetery, almost a physical link . . . She would rather keep all that side of things out of their pleasant meetings. She told herself that it had never been her policy to mix business and private matters. The graveplot, though large and with room still to spare, was not a distinctive one and was fortunately in the most deeply wooded part. The cemetery records had been destroyed by a timely incendiary bomb near London Wall in 1940.

They were still on Dinshaw-Thacker. Someone was suggesting approaching the Calcutta Cricket Club for financial support. Mr Tobin, having made his unusual contribution, had apparently lost interest. He was sketching a nice little eighteenth-century doorway in the margin of the agenda, carefully shading the fanlight. She watched with pleasure as he began to add a house round it.

Nigel had talked of being an architect, as he had talked of many things that, in the event, he had not had time to accomplish. 'Such a gifted, promising boy,' an old friend of the family had written to their father after Nigel had been killed in that terrible car-crash. Their father had kept that letter till his own death, but afterwards, clearing out the family house, she had burnt it. She remembered the emotions with which she had watched it flame. *Hindus burn their dead.* It hadn't made any difference, though.

45

She must have missed something, for they were apparently on to Item 6a now, the mortuary chapel, an unsafe structure whose fate hung, in several senses, in the balance. The council wanted to demolish it; the D. of E., however, were thought to favour its restoration on historical grounds. Reassured that this delicate balance showed, for the moment, no sign of being upset, Mary returned to her private, obsessing theme.

One reason why she had never mentioned in committee that Nigel (and her parents of course) were in the cemetery was that the people round the table would misunderstand. With a quickness born of an under-exercised intelligence and a lifetime of reading novels, she could see all too clearly how *they* would see it: the lonely but plucky old maid, still after fifty years mourning her only brother . . . the shared childhood . . . the young life cut short . . . the Golden Boy in his red roadster . . . the slim volume of poetry he had published only the year before . . . the humorous sketches . . . the heart-broken testimonials from god-parents, teachers and old school-friends . . . Even the fact that he had died with a girl in the car who was unknown to anyone but who proved to be the daughter of a publican in Hayling might, at a distance of fifty years, be interpreted as a poignant and romantic circumstances . . . young love . . . the runaway passion that brooked no denying . . .

Mary made a face and consciously pulled herself together. That was really a little too much: she never read *that* sort of novel, after all. Young love indeed! You really were getting old when you assumed young love to be naturally romantic and pure. She recalled the couples from the East Woodgate Comprehensive School who were said to break into the cemetery at night and 'copulate' on the graves, and again she felt that bracing charge of emotion she had felt when she burnt the letter Father had kept.

But it was no good. He would just have laughed. His throat, rising from a white cricket shirt, elongated and almost girlish as in the pastel sketch of him that had been in Mother's bedroom. Young for ever . . . Dust to dust. How sorry the Committee would be if they knew that so much

46

youth and strength and gaiety had just been put away under the ground. It would not occur to them to take any other view.

Young for ever. But he had only been a year younger than she. Now he would be an elderly man, slow and craven, perhaps, like the rest of them round this table. She looked at their receding hair or frankly bald heads, at their bloodshot eyes and weathered cheeks, at their jowls and their stringy necks and at the liver-coloured patches on their hands. And her train of thought ended, as it always ended, in a sense of frustration, the realisation once again that age shall not wither Nigel nor the years condemn . . . Young for ever.

The secretary was reading out some estimates for the repair of the boundary walls (Item 6*b*). The sums of money sounded absurdly enormous. Surely it couldn't cost all that just to rebuild some brickwork? But the several architects present appeared to be contemplating the sums with placidity, even with complacence. Of course the architect's fee was normally, or so she understood, a percentage of the total costs . . . But no, it was out of the question to think of any of the Committee in that light: people of the highest probity and scruples all of them. All the same, no wonder architects seemed to earn a lot.

Nigel would no doubt have earned a lot – if his ideas about architecture had ever come to anything. In fact, now she came to think about it, it might have been the ideal occupation for him, with his many gifts: his enterprise, his flair for making strangers like him, his quickness at sensing any new trend, his talent for sketching . . .

. . . His fondness for grandiose schemes at other people's expense, his glib virtuosity, his weakness for anything new and contempt for anything old, his essential destructiveness. *How* he would have enjoyed destroying the old cemetery, and indeed the whole of Woodgate Village, and putting other things in their place. Yes, in the twentieth century, architecture or town planning would have been a very suitable occupation for him.

(Mr Rammage was remarking that the council might be

47

persuaded to shell out more money for the boundary walls if a big enough stink about break-ins and vandalism were raised in the local Press. Come to that, the national Press might stir their stumps if they thought the story was juicy enough. At this, several people round the table looked nervous, and one lady remarked rather sharply after a slight pause that surely lurid publicity was the *last* thing they wanted?)

Cruel, thought Mary relentlessly: he was cruel, he despised us all, even Father. The fights they used to have . . . And the way he bullied me all through our childhood and teens, even though he was the younger, demonstrating to me over and over and over again that he was the clever one, the master, and that I was a poor, muddle-headed, sentimental creature incapable of logical thought or efficient action. Well, Nigel, I've spent my life proving that you were wrong: I've turned myself, over the decades, into efficient, sensible Miss Spencer-Byrd. I never married the flabby fool you predicted for me. I've long ago given up the ready tears which you portrayed again and again in those cruel, beastly drawings you used to do. You were wrong, Nigel. In spite of all your cleverness you were wrong, and I have proved it.

The last thing he ever said to me, the very last thing as he was dressing to go out that night, was: 'Mary, if you tell the parents about Dolly I'll make damn sure you're sorry. I'm warning you!' And I didn't tell, because I was a coward in those days, and when the police came at midnight and told us about the crash my first thought was: *Who's sorry now?* They were the words of a popular song then, and they fitted so perfectly.

But of course the dead aren't sorry, because they don't know enough to be. It's time and knowledge that make you sorry about things, and the dead are safe from time and knowledge. The dead are secure.

How he would hate the idea that he's just one more body in a picturesque old graveyard which no one must touch or alter! I tell myself that . . . And yet, just as when I burnt that fulsome, sentimental letter about him, I don't feel that

48

much triumph; I don't feel I have really got the better of him. For he's young and he's dead and therefore beyond reach. You won, Nigel, you won – though almost every day in the last fifty years I have done some little thing or other in an attempt to prove to myself that you did not. *'Where is death's sting? Where, grave, thy victory?'* When grandfather Spencer had that carved on the stone for his wife in 1892 he can never have imagined what a bitter interpretation the words might have.

(The estimates for the boundary walls were still being discussed. The general feeling of the meeting was that some work must be done soon, even of a provisional nature, in view of the 'incursions' by tramps and teenagers. Mr Rammage also mentioned the words '. . . like a public lavatory' in tones of explosive disgust.)

Nigel would have enjoyed baiting Mr Rammage. Come to that, he would have enjoyed what was happening in the cemetery these days; it was just the sort of sordid, distressing thing that he found funny. It must be stopped. Copulating on the graves, indeed! He'd have drawn dirty pictures of it. That private sketch-book of his I found after his death . . .

She raised her hand:

'Mr Chairman, I should like to endorse most strongly this recommendation about work being done *pro tem* to make the cemetery more secure. After all, apart from the question of possible damage to monuments, I feel that it is our first duty to ensure that the peaceful character of the place is maintained. Surely we owe that at least to the dead – before we can begin to consider the needs of the living?'

The murmur of acquiescence round the table reassured her.

Going Home I

I've never been much of a one for guided tours or indeed
package holidays at all. However, since I have become a
widower such things have seemed a solution, of a sort. It's
ironic that, during all our years together, it was Marjorie
who was the keener on going to places, while I used to put in
pleas for staying at home and enjoying the garden while it
was at its best. But you can't just enjoy the garden on your
own, can you? I can't, anyway. And since the annual
holiday comes round whether you want it to or not . . . In
another few years, when I'm sixty-five, it'll be holiday all
the time. I don't much enjoy thinking about that, I must
confess.

Anyway, with Marjorie in charge we did end up going to
some nice places, which have at least given me happy
memories: the Lake District, Ireland once, Spain of course,
Italy (which I didn't like much), Malta my favourite, and
Corfu which I liked very much also though I hadn't
expected to. Of course Corfu was British at one time too.
Nowhere really adventurous, you might say, but that was
because Marjorie herself wasn't keen on long plane
journeys. Even before her illness she had trouble with
swelling fingers and ankles. It's strange to think that,
though she was the real traveller of the two of us, if she had
lived we would almost certainly never have come here.
Fourteen hours in a jet plane, even with a stop in some Gulf
airport in the middle of the night, is no joke. Still, as my
travel agent said, for an all-in package deal it's wonderful
value. The luxury of the hotel is really extraordinary – great
marble halls, air-conditioning throughout, complete room
service, a choice of four restaurants . . . Apparently the
Government here has over-extended itself on hotel building
these last few years and is now rather desperate to fill all this
accommodation. Hence the hordes of Australians in the

marble halls, noisily present on all the coach tours, no doubt all with package deals comparable to mine. I wish I liked Australians better. Certainly they've every bit as much right here today as I have.

Perhaps I should have known better than to go on all the tours, even though they are included in the price. But, when I venture out into the town on my own I feel so lost – quite literally lost. It's unnerving. You think for a few minutes that you know where you are, and then . . . Anyway, the trip to the bird-park was nice: I enjoyed that, wonderful trees and flowers too. And yesterday's tour out to the countryside sounded good in prospect. What I should have realised, however, is that, with the developments of the last twenty years, there's hardly any real countryside left on the island of Singapore any more, just ring-roads and parks and suburbs and yet more suburbs, all delightfully, tropically green but somehow like a stage set rather than a place with a life of its own. They took us to a *kampong* –well, they called it that, but the little group of houses on their traditional stilts seemed to me to have been heavily sanitised, and whatever the original occupation of the people their present one was selling beer, Coca-Cola and knick-knacks to the likes of my Australian companions. I suppose in honesty I should say 'to the likes of me', for am I not just as much a tourist as they are? But I don't want knick-knacks, particularly manufactured 'handicrafts' in straw and plastic, and I don't like having cans of drinks thrust on me. It embarrassed me to have these local people ingratiatingly 'inviting' me into their homes like especially well-trained animals in a zoo.

We went to a zoo too, in the course of that aching afternoon, or rather to a crocodile and alligator farm. I tried to summon up some interest in that because after all that's a manufacturing industry and one is always glad to hear of a place like this selling something more solid than tourism. However, I have never much enjoyed seeing creatures imprisoned, even crocodiles, and the tiny, dreary pools in their cement pits seemed such a desolate mockery of the great, up-country rivers from which these beasts must have come. Like the Malays of the *kampong* they seemed to have had their real life taken away from them.

I suppose I was hardly in the mood for the crocodile farm – and certainly not for buying an expensive handbag in the shop where we were forced to loiter interminably, prisoners ourselves of the tour-operator. (To whom would I give such a handbag anyway?) Because, by that stage in the tour, we had already been conducted round an actual prison. That, for me, had been the point of the day.

Changi Jail. Most of the tour companies seem to include it on their itineraries. There were other coaches besides our own in the car park, and groups of other but identical Europeans and Australians being led about all over the place. Must be very odd being an inmate of the jail these days with all this spectator activity going on. I suggested just now that the crocodile zoo was like a prison, but it is equally true that the prison was like a zoo. The peculiar thing is that of course it is full of ordinary criminals – thieves, drug-pushers and so on – like any jail anywhere, but that isn't why the public are allowed into it. Oh, no doubt whoever that chap is who's in charge of Singapore these days likes to demonstrate that he's not afraid to let foreigners visit his jail – that he's nothing particular to hide. But the reason tourists are shovelled off there in bus-loads is not to bear witness to a humane regime or yet to boost the jail's finances by buying expensive soft-drinks in the waiting area. It's because the jail's got a memorial chapel which was set up after the War. That's why the British, and the Australians, get taken there. Not that there's anything particularly historical about it, bar the photos. It isn't even, as far as I could gather, the room that was used as a chapel at the time. It's a gesture, that's what it is – though I don't mean it isn't a decent one. A small marker for the past in the city that has changed so much since the 1940s as to be totally unrecognisable.

But the jail itself is still the same building: built by the British themselves before the War – what an irony. Anyway, after our coach had called there I was more or less finished for the day with *kampongs* or crocodile farms or

53

anything else, particularly with repulsive handicrafts and 'have-a-nice-beer'. I just wanted to be by myself to think a bit, and of course that was the one thing I couldn't have. In the end I left everybody else mooching around crocodile-skin shoes or alligator foetuses pickled in glass jars (each to his taste) and went and sat by myself in the back of the coach. And, yes, I gave myself up to the sin of hate, hating the coach, the crocodile farm, the Australians, the silly Chinese tour-guide and his cleft palate speech (but he was only doing his job, poor little sod, and lucky to have it no doubt) – hating the whole clear, bright, multinational, high-rise city and its genteel hinterland which had swallowed irretrievably what once had been. And hating myself too, for having been so stupid as to come here at all. I should have had the sense to stay at home.

Home – where is home? Five thousand miles away in the house in Esher that is still full of Marjorie, but where Marjorie will never be again? Or somewhere else entirely, infinitely less accessible?

By and by I moved from hate to reverie, a better state perhaps. So that I was deep in Changi Jail again when the coach refilled with sweaty T-shirts and pink thighs, and the man who had the misfortune of a seat next to mine asked me, with despairing conviviality, 'Been here before, have you?'

I suppose he meant, had I been to the crocodile farm before? (In other words, was that why I was being so snooty about it?) Or maybe he just meant had I been in Singapore before? But, imprisoned in my reverie, I thought he meant Changi, and snapped back, 'No – no, never before. Once is enough, I'd say.'

Unknown Australian, I offer you an apology. I have been here before. In fact, I was born here. This, you may say, was my home, indisputably, once.

We lived in a little house out at Katong on the eastern side of the city, Mummy, Daddy and me. In those days it was a separate township set in a countryside of plantations and rice-paddies – a village really, but with a fringe of

European-style bungalows like ours, built I suppose between the wars when the tramline came out from the city. The old airport, where the planes with propellers used to take off, was out that way too: one of our amusements on Sundays was to sit in the garden and watch with binoculars as the planes rose into the warm air. How innocent and futile that now sounds, and how happy we were.

We drove past Katong yesterday on our way to Changi. The tour-guide pointed out to us that the old runway had become part of Singapore's ring-road system; otherwise, I should never have known it. Katong itself had new air-conditioned shopping centres along the main highway, and rows of sea-food restaurants. Most of the old-style houses had gone. The bigger private gardens, and the fields and plantations in between, were filled with other buildings, or else there were notices saying things like 'Ho Lee Investment Pte Ltd' or 'Two-storey split-level semi-detached' or 'Spanish-style magnificent, spacious interiors'. Spanish style? Here? The Spaniards never came, I think, to this swampy tip of Malaya, nor even the sea-faring Portuguese. Only gentleman Raffles came, and after him the ubiquitous Chinese traders.

As a small boy I did not properly realise that my father was yet another in the long train of men who have traditionally come from the far side of the world to Singapore to seek their fortunes. However, though that may have been literally true, it is far too grandiose and romantic a designation for a modest man like Daddy. Yet coming as he did from Birmingham, and from the family of a Board School teacher with too many children, Singapore must indeed have seemed to him a paradise of light and colour. He made it his home. He worked for the Hong Kong-Shanghai Bank, the big branch in Orchard Road. It was a good job: he was proud of it – or at any rate Mummy was. Just occasionally, in the holidays from school, Mummy and I would take the long tramride into town, and then a bus up to Orchard Road. There we would pop into a dress-shop or two – Chinese shop-houses, they were of course in those days, with work-rooms behind the

55

front shop – and, for a treat, have a sandwich for lunch at the Cold Store. Then, for fun, we would visit Daddy behind his cash desk in the great, high banking hall with the turning fans. (That's gone now too. I looked. The bank is a new skyscraper.) Daddy would be very dignified and distant and pretend hardly to know us, though smiling at us out of the corner of his eye, and Mummy and I would laugh about it together as we walked down the hill again in the gentle, humid afternoon to catch the tram from Market Road.

And I thought, in my youth and my innocence, that everyone was as happy as we were. In those days – I am talking now, I suppose, of 1939, 1940 – Singapore had many poor people and a large population with no homes of their own. Though it is often wet in Singapore it is never ever cold, and these people used to live and sleep under the arcades of the shop-houses. As a little boy I imagined that they lived there from choice, because it was jolly and convenient, or perhaps even that the shop-houses were built that way on purpose to shelter them. It never occurred to me that they eked out their existence there from necessity, just as it never for one second occurred to me that there was any reason for Daddy, Mummy and me to live in Singapore except that it was the nicest place on earth to be. True, Daddy often told me what a wonderful place England was, but I had never yet been there. We often talked of the great trip we would all make Home, but somehow it was put off from year to year – and then the War came.

Not, at first, that the War touched Singapore. It was Over There, in Europe, thousands of miles away. There, it seemed, men floundered in mud, there great navies of 'ironclads' as in my picture-books battled in mysteriously grey and storm-lashed seas as in a permanent typhoon. (These images seem, on reflection, to have been borrowed from an earlier war, but it was all the same to me.) There, improbably great cities – 'larger even than Singapore' – were being flattened by bombs. But none of it meant much to me because, of course, Singapore would never be taken, even if anyone bothered to come all that way to take it.

The main and exciting difference to life, as far as I was concerned, was that Singapore filled with soldiers. By late 1941 it was also, I now know, filling steadily with refugees from further north in the Malay peninsula. The Japanese had joined in the War on Germany's side, but, even if I knew that, the geographical significance of this fact escaped me. Indeed, it seems to have escaped a lot of people. Singapore was a fortress; everyone knew that, and here was the British Army, and a part of the Navy, to prove it.

By and by Daddy joined the British Army himself as a Special Reserve Officer. Mummy was awfully proud of him in his new uniform and I assumed that he'd been specially picked out to serve because people high up in the Army realised what a fine soldier he would make. Perhaps a general had come into the bank to cash a cheque and had got talking to him? Today, when I am far older than he was ever destined to be, if no wiser, it occurs to me that the war represented a chance for Daddy, as for many other people of undistinguished social background. Had he been able to make his mark as an officer he might have gone quite far, farther at any rate than he would ever have got in the bank in those days, since he was married to Mummy. Promotion stopped for men who made mistakes of that kind. Somehow, in spite of admiring them both so much, I knew that, though I can't imagine that anyone had ever spelt it out to me. Even a child, insulated in kindness and security, can know complex things without properly putting them into words.

Mummy was what used to be called 'Straits born'. Of course there were other, ruder words, but we never dreamed of using any of them in our house. I knew them all, from the playground at school, but somehow they just rolled off me. I never applied them to Mummy, even in my mind. I was too well loved.

Sometimes, on Sundays, we used to pack delicious things into the picnic basket and get the train from the old station that's now gone, across the Causeway to the mainland of Malaya. There were lovely beaches up there . . . It's no use. I cannot remember in any personal way, however hard

57

I try, the sequence of events by which this idyllic life was brought to an end. Adult knowledge, acquired many years later, tells me that by Christmas 1941 the Japanese were moving rapidly down Malaya, marching on Fortress Singapore in its vulnerable rear, circumventing and cutting off the British Army detachments that were sent too late – always too late – to stop them. Did this fatal tardiness and unawareness affect Daddy too, as he sat at his new military desk job near Raffles Hotel? Surely there must have been, for him as for others, a panic-stricken period of knowing that Singapore was about to fall and, with it, the knowledge that it was now too late to take any of the steps that might have been taken before?

But I cannot recapture this period. For me, in memory, it is as if one Sunday we were riding in a train over the Causeway, over the shining water, picnic on our laps and cheerful expectation in our hearts, and the very next one we were standing, cases in hand, in a heaving queue at the docks, while gunfire sounded from the north of the city and bombed rubber warehouses burnt themselves out near at hand in a choking cloud of black smoke.

At last, after a great many queues and some frightening scenes, Mummy and I were somehow taken on a crowded Dutch ship bound for Bombay. Perhaps the Hong Kong-Shanghai Bank tried, after all, to do a good turn for its own. From Bombay we were taken, eventually, to England.

I had heard so much about England, and when we docked in a Portsmouth already itself rendered ugly with bomb-damage, and walked with our cases under a cold drizzle to the Refugee Reception Centre to which we were designated, something – faith, hope or perhaps just innocence – died in me. Home. Was this 'home'? No, my mind protested, there was surely some dreadful mistake. It wasn't that anything particularly horrible happened to us – nothing like those last days and nights on the docks at Singapore. People were preoccupied and tired but not positively unfriendly. We did not starve. Shabby second-hand overcoats were even given to us. A residential

58

domestic job was found for Mummy where she could have me with her. We settled down. Only, nothing was ever the same again. How could it be?

Since then, England has given me my education, my National Service, my career, my marriage, a few friends, my house in Esher – my whole life. And yet, and yet . . . For many years Singapore remained in my mind as something almost intolerably bright and real against which all these other English things would eventually have to be compared. But of course the moment of comparison never came; Singapore dwindled to a painful stab of colour at which I never looked. And now, at the other end of time, I realise it can never be anything more than that because the Singapore which was the original real life to me exists nowhere any more.

Mummy died while I was doing my National Service. She'd never really settled down in England and her last years must have been saddened by the awareness that I was growing away from her as I had to, an alien young man in an alien country. Yet perhaps all children have to become aliens to their parents at some level as part of their necessary growing up? I wouldn't know. Marjorie and I never had any children. Perhaps it's just as well.

The British, both military and civilian, who were caught in Singapore when the Japs arrived, were interned in Changi Jail. So were quite a few Australian troops who had been landed in Singapore (too late, of course) to help defend the island. In Changi, I have read, people were crowded into mass cells where they had to sit on the floor from eight in the morning till late into the night with their backs straight, their knees up and their hands clasped together. They were beaten if they moved for any reason other than to go to the lavatory, and sometimes beaten in any case. There was one open lavatory bowl per cell. Everyone had dysentery. There was a starvation diet of watery soup. I realise I have led a sheltered life myself, but I just don't know how people can stand their existence under such conditions. Evidently Daddy couldn't, for he died there, in Changi. We only heard that afterwards, when the war was over.

59

During those years as a schoolboy in England, when Mummy and I still talked about Singapore, I used to play a game with myself, shutting my eyes and making believe for a moment that England and everything associated with it had disappeared like a dream, and that the real place was Singapore and that I only had to open my eyes again to see it. I played the game so hard that once or twice I almost believed it must work. (It never did.)

Now, since I became a widower, I play something like that game again. Well, not exactly because I don't make efforts about it on purpose: I don't shut my eyes. But perhaps I play it in sleep, because sometimes I wake, confused, thinking: Was that a dream, the idea that Marjorie might be gone? . . .

Or was the dream all those years with her?

Going Home II

Waking soon after dawn, Judith got up to drink some water from the hygienically-cooled flask and to pull the curtain a little aside. She looked down from the sealed window. Beyond the double glass, many floors below, the scene seemed as remote as a rather uninteresting film, sounds and scents all absent. Delhi lay cloudy in the distance, any great city, not specifically Indian. Immediately below, in the hotel car park, taxis slept in black and yellow wasp rows. Between the hotel and an indeterminate middle ground of scrub land dotted with a few buildings lay the wide perimeter road that led to the airport. At this early hour there was already a little traffic, moving toys from where she stood: a lorry or two of old-fashioned shape, an Army vehicle, the occasional car. She stood hoping for a buffalo cart, but none appeared: perhaps carts did not bring vegetables into the cities any more?

Then, slowly along the road, came a fragile bicycle, pedalled by the usual thin, dark man. It was pulling a cart, on which was a large sack, a bundle of rods which might have been metal or bamboo, and two other men.

As she watched, marvelling at the rider's endurance, he stopped and seemed to argue with the two men who were getting a lift. At any rate one of them got off to walk. The contraption slowly moved on again. She watched it, craning her neck, till it passed beyond her field of vision. In that unplace, in which she found herself poised, it seemed the only object by which she could connect herself to earth.

She was suspended in a de luxe international hotel, marbled halls like a palace or a temple, complete with young, smiling, well-trained acolytes of both sexes who called you 'Ma'am' and asked you to have a nice day. Not for this recently-built Taj-Hilton-Oberoi (or whatever it

61

was) the elderly, barefoot, gap-toothed servants in crumpled white or khaki cotton that she had known long ago.

'Bloody inconvenient,' her husband had said in a disgruntled tone, 'being stuck right out here. I just hope the Company's got a decent discount this time.' It had been she who had replied soothingly:

'Oh, come on, let's enjoy it while we're here. It's only for a few days. And there's a lovely pool . . .'

But it was he, now, lulled into good humour by a large, delicious dinner and assiduous service, who lay peacefully sleeping, and she who had passed a confused, even anguished night.

Hours later, when she had breakfasted in bed like an invalid because it seemed expected, and her husband had disappeared to his meeting in some unknown hinterland, she, not knowing what else to do and not recognising herself in this unaccustomed idleness, ventured out to the pool. It lay in full sun, a Spanish-holiday style anachronism in a land of people dedicated to seeking shade. She recoiled in instinctive shock, remembering the drawn blinds and hats of her childhood, the shadowed verandahs, the constant exhortations not to expose herself to the glare of the day because she would surely get sunstroke. Europeans always did, it appeared. Indians, of course, were quite different.

Yet here by the pool lay several almost naked European women – Company wives of various kinds like herself, she supposed, with another tiny shock of realising this new role. Two heavy women conversing in – Dutch, was it? – nearest to her seemed to be turning salmon-coloured already. One wore a one-piece costume firm with bones, but the other was covered only in tiny triangles of cloth attached here and there by strings. She was apparently oblivious of the amount of flaccid flesh she was exposing. Shocked in some part of herself that seemed to be located far back in time and not to be in adequate communication with her present self, Judith thought, 'Stupid cow – so unsuitable here – serve her right if she gets an awful burn.' And then thought, 'Why be so censorious? The young waiters here must be used to it, and what harm is she doing? She's simply relaxing by the pool, like the hotel brochure says you're supposed to, like you told James you were going to yourself. Who are you to criticise?'

She found a patch of shade at a table with an umbrella and asked one of the boys for a *nimbopani*. The phrase, unused for decades, had suddenly appeared on her tongue.

She tried to read. She had brought a number of solid books with her, telling herself that the unprecedented leisure of this trip with James would give her the opportunity to catch up on the background reading that, with her teaching load, she just did not get done. However, she found it difficult to concentrate. Even in the shade the heat was intense, and the presence of the other supine bodies – to the women round the pool had now been added two Japanese men – was not conducive to thinking about Jane Austen's moral realism. It was a newish biography, by one of those efficient American academics one heard were so well paid . . . He came from California, the book jacket said: perhaps, in spite of Jane Austen, he would have known better than she did how to use this pool, how to talk to the other women sunning themselves. Other people, she had noticed, were often so much better than she herself at slipping in and out of different identities, adapting themselves.

The Japanese, having disported themselves athletically in the water, ordered beer and sandwiches. She ordered another lime and soda and (they looked so good) a sandwich too. She felt vaguely guilty at such self-indulgence mid-morning – but, after all, it had been she who had said to James, 'Let's enjoy it while we're here.' She was simply behaving as a Company wife was supposed to behave . . . Did they lie here *all* day, she wondered?

No, probably in the afternoon they went and had their hair done at the shop in the foyer in preparation for an evening function. 'Isn't it bliss, my dear?' she had just heard one English voice say to another.

Bliss? Doing nothing under the pitiless sun. Being waited on by young Hindus who must – certainly – despise you in their hearts for several reasons. Bliss?

Then she thought again: why, why so critical? They are just ordinary wives like yourself – a little richer, perhaps, less bookish, that's all. At home in Basingstoke or wherever they too have to contend with many of the trials and pains of real life: why begrudge them their bliss just because they find it so easily?

When the sandwich and drink came, and the chit to sign for them, she hardly dared look at the price. It seemed enormous. But James was obviously not going to fuss. Not this trip.

In her childhood they had counted in annas. Sixteen annas to the rupee. Now the anna had disappeared; the rupee was decimalised, and anyway seemed hardly worth dividing into fractions any more. Or was it only in a place like this hotel that a single rupee was so insignificant, not really enough to give as a tip, she and James had thought. Perhaps in the streets the people still used tiny coins. She had not yet been beyond the confines of the hotel. It was not India that intimidated her – how could it? No, it was that main road, the impression of being nowhere.

In the little house in the Railway Colony money was not wasted, nothing was wasted. They had had one servant who, far from being ignored as a blissful convenience, was constantly watched, exhorted, suspected. For those years Daddy was away, a prisoner of war with the wicked Japs in Burma, and though Mummy still got his Army pay, of course, she was worried that he might never come home again. Mummy and Judith had led a quiet and economical life, keeping themselves to themselves, associating with no one much but Auntie next door, who was not a real aunt but a lady called Mrs Da Souza. They could have gone on living on the cantonment at Meerut while waiting for Daddy to come home again, but Mummy had preferred to come down to Delhi to be closer to Grandma and Pa. But both of them had died in 1942; Mummy and Judith finished the war in Delhi alone.

Mummy didn't like to associate much with other officers' wives. She said it didn't do to be too familiar with other people; that they got to know too much about your business. Only years later, long after Mummy was dead, did Judith come to comprehend what this meant.

Apparently being familiar with Mrs Da Souza didn't count.

Mummy had grown up in Delhi. Yes. But, as the war neared its end and it became possible to hope that Daddy might really be coming back after all, Mummy began telling Judith to say her family had come from near Brighton, Sussex, UK. It couldn't be quite true, not in the way other things were true, or why shouldn't Mummy have said so before? And Mummy didn't seem to remember anything about Brighton except that it was a large town near the sea. But it was clearly important to Mummy that it should be true in some way, and Judith had tried hard to believe it.

All so long ago. Dead, finished, over, nothing to be frightened of any more. She was here by a blue pool, eating an expensive sandwich, surrounded by strangers, and that was *all*. 'It'll be interesting for you, going back to India,' James had said. 'Delhi too – you'll be able to look up some of your old haunts.' But she had just said, 'Oh, I may not bother . . . There's no one there now. And I expect Delhi's changed a lot.'

Was Mrs Da Souza still there? Old and poor, perhaps, in some crumbling block impregnated with the neighbours' alien garlic and asafoetida and the miasma of poor drainage, where Hindi film music blared all day? Irrecoverable . . .

She had never told James about Mrs Da Souza. Actually she had never told him about the little house in the Railway Colony either, or about what had happened to Mummy. All he knew was that Judith's father, who had died before their marriage, had been a British Army officer who was stationed in India at the outbreak of war: James was not a curious man.

If he *had* known about Mummy – anything about Mummy – he probably wouldn't have minded. For an uncertain-tempered man he was remarkably easy about things which, as he said, did not concern him. But not telling anyone – anything – about Mummy had become such a habit with Judith that she could not break it. Not with James. Not even with the children. No one.

She finished her sandwich and put her sunglasses back on. Under the umbrella she did not really need them, but she felt safer behind them.

One of the muscular Japanese had left his sandwich unattended and was back in the pool. She noticed this when she saw the inevitable raven circle, land, and approach the appetising object. Black and glossy, clearly thriving in a country where so many failed to thrive, it eyed the sandwich speculatively and then began to pull at it, testing its weight. Too far away to have shooed it off in time, Judith watched with interest and amusement: she had always liked ravens, though her mother had said they were horrible birds.

Evidently deciding that the sandwich was more than it could manage on its own, the raven flapped off over the hedge of tamarind that marked the back of the hotel compound, and shortly reappeared with another raven. Using their powerful curved beaks and prehensile claws, the two birds divided the food between them and flew away with their booty beyond the hedge, just as a bearer rushed angrily up to the table.

After a few minutes Judith went to look over the hedge herself. The ravens had disappeared, presumably to take their goods off to their own eyrie in a tree. The green, post-monsoon scrub stretched away: by Christmas it would be brown and dusty again. But she now saw for the first time that, half hidden among the bushes, two or three hundred yards off was a collection of shanties, not proper huts but awful makeshift ones: tin roofs, sheets of plastic or rag, litter, stray dogs, small dirty children . . .

This was probably where many of the hotel servants lived. Not the smart bearers in their Kashmiri uniforms but the cleaners, the kitchen boys.

Of course in her childhood people like her and Mummy and Mrs Da Souza had never worried particularly about the poor people, such as lived down by the railway tracks. Indians were like that. They didn't mind such conditions.

One should accept the vast differences that existed. The world was a big place.

Two opposing life-views warred within her, a kind of mental double vision that seemed to be making her head ache. Or was it just the sun?

She went indoors and lay down in the hermetically cooled bedroom, and tried again without success to be interested in Jane Austen.

When she woke it was nearly three. A sudden sense of urgency replaced her previous emptiness. James would be back some time after six, full of how his meeting had been, and so far she herself had done nothing – nothing to justify coming all this way to India, nothing to justify her existence. That was awful.

She washed, tidied her hair, and went down to the palatial ground floor. Two tiny girls in tunics and trousers were playing tag with a still smaller boy among the low, stuffed sofas and glass tables of the lounge area. A notice said: 'Today – Mezzanine Conference Suite: Sweetie weds Sanjay.' The *chowkidar* called a taxi as soon as she appeared on the steps outside – of course, no visitor could go anywhere from here except by taxi – and, all in a moment it seemed, she was on that desolate ring-road and moving towards Delhi.

She had asked for Connaught Circus simply as a central place to name, but now she changed her mind.

'Driver – Imperial Hotel.'

He waggled his head in the archetypal Indian acknowledgment.

When the war was over and Daddy had come back, very thin but, as he said, reasonably fit in spite of the Japs, his blue eyes bright in his sunburnt face and his hair bleached and sparse, they had often gone to the Imperial. It was the favourite place for British officers and their families to go. The big, old-fashioned bar was full of smart khaki and Sam Brownes. On the garden terrace wives in bright cotton frocks drank tea or gin and tonic according to the hour, and pale, imperious children played noisily on the grass, teasing

67

the *malis* and running through the spray from the hoses. After dark, the big ballroom began to fill. Judith had loved the Imperial; sitting there in her best white frock, drinking *nimbopani* and being introduced to people Daddy knew, was such fun, much, much more fun than being at home. It irritated her when Mummy didn't want to go and made excuses about headaches, and she could see it irritated Daddy too. Sometimes she overheard them:

'Oh, come on Nancy, what are you fussing about? It'll be just the Baileys and the Grant-Wests and a few others of the crowd.'

'Mrs Grant-West doesn't like me.'

'Oh, go on, of course she does. Why shouldn't she? You must just chat to her in an ordinary, relaxed way, I've told you that before. And anyway, what does it matter what Sally Grant-West thinks?'

But it did matter, Judith knew that. And she knew that her father really thought so too. She had sensed his tension, his restiveness, when Mummy either talked too much or stayed sulkily silent. There was something wrong with Mummy. Judith knew that herself. But she did not yet know what it was.

By and by Mummy had almost stopped coming to the Imperial at all.

'Why should I come just for Daddy's friends to look down on me?'

'They don't, Mummy, don't be silly.' But Judith knew they did.

'You must pull yourself together when we get Home, Nancy', Daddy used to say. He had got annoyed with her now, and no longer tried to cheer her up. 'Home' meant England. London and Brighton and Lincolnshire (where Daddy had grown up) and all those other places. In England there were food shortages and it was wet and cold most of the time and white men swept the streets. It didn't sound much fun, thought Judith. But that wasn't why Mummy didn't want to go there, now it came to it, in spite of her talk about Brighton.

One night when she was supposed to be asleep, Judith

heard Mommy crying and crying and saying that Daddy didn't really want her to come back Home with him at all – that Daddy was ashamed of her.

Daddy didn't deny it, as Judith thought he should have done. He must have been in a bad temper, because he just said:

'Have it your own way, Nancy. *Don't* come then, if you don't want to. But I warn you, Judith's coming with me.'

Hearing that, she had been filled with a secret, guilty delight that Daddy liked her more than he did Mummy. He often said what good company she was. But by and by Daddy went out, and Mummy was still crying and Judith felt so dreadfully sorry for her that she began to cry a little herself. She got up and crept into her parents' bedroom and snuggled on to the bed beside her mother. Mummy had lovely black hair, not really long of course but all permed and pretty, and her skin smelt to Judith like no one else's.

But the Judith of the present was arriving at the Imperial. The portly Sikh doorman – could it still be the same one? – opened the taxi door.

In spite of that last time there, the Judith-of-the-past who seemed to be living inside her felt the old tremor of pleasure and excitement as she wandered into the long hall. And in the lounge and on the terrace would be nice British officers and their wives . . .

But as soon as she was fully inside she realised that it had changed. Of course it had, in forty years. Not much, but significantly. There were more shops and booths and notices for travel agents. And passing down the hall, as well as lots of Indians, were some very ordinary-looking European tourists hung with cameras, in short and awful sun dresses, and even a little group of what looked like sub-hippies, English or American – one man with a beard, another wearing some sort of native dress, and an untidy girl in a long skirt.

Yet the Imperial had been the best hotel in town. That's why Daddy and all the others had come here, that's why it had been the end of Mummy.

Only now of course it had probably been overtaken by

69

the new five-star hotels like the one she and James were staying in. And anyway tourists and hippies got everywhere, now.

She found her way to the lounge which, with its carpet and plush furniture, still seemed the same as ever, but deserted and melancholy. She ordered a pot of tea.

Mummy had always been peremptory with the servants. Daddy, however, had said 'Please' and 'Thank you' and had told Judith to do so as well, explaining that she must get into the habit because in England you must be polite to everyone 'particularly these days'. Mummy had been right, of course – you don't say 'Please' to servants in India – but being right in that kind of way had not done poor Mummy any good.

Her tea was slowly drunk. She asked for more hot water, read a *Times of India* that was lying around. Stirs in UP, a *bandh* in Madras, a hike in vegetable prices . . . Tributes to an eminent Shri Vikram Ganpat, recently deceased . . . Applications from BAs, First Class only, welcomed by large electrical firm . . . It was no good. She could not any longer put off what she had come for, though she had not know till that moment what it was.

She poured and drank the last of her stewed tea, counted out notes and left them on the tray, folded the newspaper tidily for the next passer-by. Then she walked purposefully out of the lounge and towards the lifts.

'Which floor, madame?'

She told the attendant, 'Six'. No one would query her presence on the upper floors of the hotel. She was a British lady.

At the far end of the sixth floor, walking slowly between rows of doors as if she were tired from shopping and knew quite well where she was going, she found the other lift and, by it, what she was seeking: a tall window looking down on to the compound. It was at the side of the hotel: from it, she could see servants trailing around with cloths over their shoulders; a squat washerman went by with a huge head-load done up in a sheet. A cat delicately inspected a pile of coconut shells. Beyond stretched the green garden with its

70

rows of palm trees. This was much nicer than the view she had seen from the other hotel at dawn: here all was familiar, real.

The Imperial was not comprehensively air-conditioned as the new hotel was: she opened the window easily. She heard the birds talking in Hindi and a radio warbling on somewhere in the kitchen regions.

'British wife falls to death in Imperial hotel'

For a long time she hesitated.

Was this the window from which Mummy had jumped? She did not really know. And now no one would be left to remember.

It had been dreadful at the time, quite dreadful. Like a stain scorched into her memory, irremovable but obscuring detail, was the sense of horror that surrounded the event. Pain, yes, but also shame: shame and disgust and embarrassment that Mummy had let them down so. Poor Daddy. Because everyone had known, really, that it couldn't be an accident.

'Anglo-Indians may seem all right, but they're no good in a crisis . . . lose their heads . . . no backbone . . . hysterical . . .' People didn't say that sort of thing these days, but they had then.

Someone had even said, not realising Judith could hear:

'All for the best really, you know, poor woman. Alec will be able to make a fresh start . . .'

Almost at once after Mummy was dead, it seemed, Daddy and Judith had gone Home. To Aldershot. Judith had gone to boarding school near Winchester, and, by and by, Daddy had married again.

She had never allowed herself to miss her mother. If you let yourself begin on *that* . . . But for years she had missed India, chronically, unobtrusively, continually, its sights and sounds and smells like a perpetual undercover dream.

Leaving the window open, she found the stairs, descended the flights on foot. At the main entrance to the hotel another taxi was ready for her.

'Where, madame?'

'Oh – the Kashmiri Gate.'

71

It was the first name from the Old City that came to her mind. She did not want to return yet to the hotel by the airport road. She wanted to be in India.

She stopped the taxi just short of the gate, by the Red Fort. The pavement there was lined with street families, arranging bedding, washing their children, lighting small fires. The day was done, dark would soon be here with its usual Indian swiftness. As she picked her way between the encampments she smelt *dal* and spices cooking. The little stalls of the *paanwallahs* and water-sellers were surrounded by men pausing on their way home from work.

The entrance to Chandni Chowk was crowded with pedal rickshaws and their skinny boy drivers. 'Yes, *mem-sahib*, yes?' they said hopefully as she passed, since they knew a white woman must be in need of some sort of transport; but she ignored them.

She turned up Chandni Chowk, into the bazaar, and soon the warm, dusty night of the Indian city covered her from view.

The Greek Experience

Henry's wife was Greek: that was the first thing that anyone mentioning him said. An unremarkable man in himself, employed in one of those professions (accountancy? insurance?) about which no one ever asks interested questions, it was almost as if he had lighted on a Greek wife to add a vital dash of colour to an otherwise monochrome self-portrait. Not, however, that anyone would have suspected him of doing anything of the sort deliberately: he was far too honest, too unpretentious, too consistently himself to resort to such a cheap trick. Indeed his integrity, a dull thing to mention and a difficult one to portray, was in practice his great glory, an invisible yet shining aura that drew acquaintances towards him readily and bound friends to him for ever. Which, his friends occasionally agreed between themselves, made it all the odder that he had married Livia.

Livia was Greek: that was the first thing everybody knew about her. The fact also became, to Henry's most loyal associates, a kind of refuge, a means of avoiding more stringent comment or analysis.

'What's Henry's wife like?'

'Oh, she's Greek, you know.'

'Oh, I see.' Being men of simple tastes at heart, married to dull, decent girls with reddened hands and spreading figures, they were prepared to accept Greek as a quite other species, another version of humanity, to whom one's own standards, for good and ill, simply could not be applied. They were pragmatic men, without self-conceit. Their own wives did not tint their hair dark red and wear it low on their necks in a coiled bun. They did not wear expensively simple dresses in suede or woven silk, they did not cook lamb on a spit or mix yoghurt with garlic: they did not speak foreign languages. Nor did they argue with their husbands in

73

public. Being reasonable men, they therefore concluded for the most part that Greek wives were something on which they themselves were entirely unequipped to have views, and in general their own wives concurred with them in this tacit assumption. It was only the occasional wife who, very late at night, after one of Livia and Henry's little parties, would remark to her husband with sudden tartness as she pulled on her girlish nylon nightdress that really she thought Livia was a bit much sometimes. (Perhaps Livia had been holding forth to the docile company on the essential importance of cotton nightwear, on the awful vulgarity of English chain-store taste, or perhaps she had just refused, as usual, to provide white Nescafé for those to whom her cups of syrupy black Greek coffee were for ever unpalatable.) And the husband in question would say, 'Well, she wouldn't suit me, but then I daresay I wouldn't suit her either,' or simply, 'Well, she makes old Henry happy, it seems,' and climb into bed with alacrity to demonstrate his own lack of interest in the subject. None of them wanted to feel disloyal, or priggishly disapproving – and anyway Livia was so exactly the sort of woman other wives *would* feel jealous of. Or so, in their decent married innocence, they believed.

As for Henry himself, he had lived for the many years of his marriage in the bemused state of being unable to imagine either how Livia had come to choose him in the first place *or* how his life would have been had he married someone ordinary. Where would have been its savour, its colour – its pain? Reviewing his happy, humdrum child-hood and youth before the Livia era, it seemed to him that he had not been truly living then – that he could not have been, without Livia to point out to him, and occasionally to demonstrate, the violence and suppressed suffering con-cealed beneath the surface of things. Only very occasion-ally, alone and exhausted under the shower late at night (Livia thought bath tubs a dirty Western European invention), did it cross his mind, like a shadow, that he might possibly be comparable with the low-powered, suburban youth who becomes addicted to a malignant drug

74

because it adds an intensity and spurious glamour to an otherwise purposeless existence.

But that was preposterous: he was a man in his fifties, successful in his profession, respected and admired, loved even. The shadow would pass like a bad dream, and he would thankfully regain the bedroom, where, on their hard, Greek-style bed, Livia's hair and nightgown would be aureoled by the spotlight as she sat propped on one graceful elbow, reading Cavafy, or some French *nouveau roman* which (being no linguist) he was incapable of even discussing with her.

Even more rarely did he reflect that if he had married someone other than Livia – a generalised someone whom he always imagined as being like his mother, with thick hips and red goose-flesh on her neck – he might have had children or, at the least, some domestic animals. He was fond of both, himself, though without much experience to enable him to discriminate between them. But Livia had a Levantine contempt for domestic animals and considered the British in general and Henry in particular repellently sentimental on the subject. And as for children – why, the subject had never really been seriously disputed between them. He had known when he married Livia that she was far too highly strung to bear children easily, and had seen too much suffering – so she said – to wish to bring children into this world anyway. And if, in the early years when the future still stretched before him as empty and inviting as a sunlit land, he had optimistically assumed that, with time, Livia's opposition to childbearing would change and mellow – well, he had learnt otherwise now.

Livia simply did not change: that was one of her qualities. Other people's wives might grow old, fat, wrinkled, take to fancy cults or drink or hormonal depressions, but Livia remained eternally the same: slim, vigorous, demanding, and remorselessly self-aware. She seemed, indeed, to have an odd relationship with time altogether – or rather, a lack of relationship: Henry had come to understand over the years that the passing of time was simply not real to her in the way it was to other people.

75

The anguishes, grievances, and slights of years ago, as well as the joys and hopes, went on existing for Livia in a kind of perpetual present of the psyche, ready at any moment to surge forward and overwhelm today. Livia did not get over things. She did not – and this, Henry reflected humbly, was just as well – get tired of things either.

It must not be thought, however (though some of his friends were inclined to think it in their rare cynical moments), that Henry gave way to Livia on every point. He let her have everything her way in the home, of course, but then the house was all Livia had through which to express her considerable personality; it was reasonable that she should have the furniture, the décor, the music, the food, the timetable of their lives, all to her taste. For he, after all, had another world to go to, about which Livia showed no curiosity or desire to control: being Greek, she had a very clear-cut idea of what was a man's sphere and what a woman's. The gaucheness, the frigidity, the pathos, the hideous Anglo-Saxon folly of the Women's Liberation Movement was a favourite subject of hers. So Henry had his work, his own quiet, prestigious sphere, another world on which Livia did not impinge at all. Hearing tales of other men's wives who constantly phoned them at the office, or expected them to do all the week's grocery shopping on Saturday mornings, he counted himself lucky, in this and in other ways too.

Their home life was uncompromisingly Greek. Livia took a siesta every afternoon and therefore never wanted to go to bed till very late at night: indeed, they did not usually have their evening meal till ten or later. Fortunately Henry had always been able to manage on rather little sleep. Their diet at home had a puristic Hellenic quality uncontaminated by such additives as puddings and pies: all through the year Livia rigorously grilled chops over charcoal, mixed tomato salads with goat cheese and oil, produced delicious but slightly scanty dishes of pickled fish, stuffed vine leaves or taramasalata. (Hummus, which Henry rather liked and found comfortably filling, she scorned as a debased middle-eastern dish, eaten by Cypriots but no part of true Grecian cuisine.) She often told Henry how fortunate he was to be eating this simple, healthy, *good* diet rather than stuffing himself on turgid British stodge as he had done when she had first met him. She was undoubtedly right, in principle, he thought, even if her theory took no account of the considerable difference in climate between London and Athens. But what he never told her was that, since he himself found yoghurt and honey, however delicious, unsufficiently sustaining for breakfast during the week, it had been his regular practice for years to call at a small workman's café on his way from the tube to his office and have a fried egg sandwich. She would have been appalled and furious at the very idea, as well as deeply hurt.

In such ways, without fuss or obvious assertion, did Henry maintain his independence. So that when friends, mellow with ouzo and retsina, declared that Livia and Henry's flat in Bayswater was 'a little bit of Greece' and that it was as good as a trip abroad to visit them, he felt able to participate wholeheartedly in their pleasure himself. He was dimly aware that beyond their Grecian home there should have been something other than the interminable moist, traffic-clogged suburbs of the Home Counties. There should have been beaches and mountains within easy reach, open roads, high bright skies, all that stark beauty to compensate for the simple, rather comfortless, domestic style. But, not being an imaginative man, he was only dimly and theoretically aware of this. For Henry himself knew Greece only through Livia. He had never actually been there.

Most of their friends – or, rather, their acquaintances, for they had few close friends as a couple – assumed they went there every year or so. A childless couple with a good income – what could be nicer than Greece for a holiday? But of course for Livia herself it wouldn't be a holiday. For, as he had tried to explain to one or two of his own intimates, Livia, though 'Greek forever' in her own phrase, had extremely painful memories associated with Greece. The result was that she had not set foot in Greece since she was sixteen years old, over thirty years earlier.

This amazing fact she chose to keep mainly secret. Indeed on the subject of her own past, its events and its time-scale, she was as vague and ambiguous as the Delphic oracle. Even Henry was not entirely clear about the details of her family's flight from Greece sometime after the end of the Second World War. Had it been, as she usually let it be understood, the Germans who had shot her father and brother, or had it (as in another version) been the Communists in '47, murdering as they retreated after their unsuccessful uprising? And why if, as Livia had once or twice angrily insisted, her family had been passionately opposed to the Germans, had they found it necessary to leave Athens after the German defeat? At all events, some tortuous and blood-smeared rationale had led Livia and her mother to two squalid years in the late 1940s in a displaced persons' camp near Trieste, in Yugoslavia ('full of dreadful Slavs, and Albanians and people who *said* they were Italian'). There, or later – the account was again unclear – her mother died, and in the following years Livia travelled, improbably, via Paris to Bournemouth, where she worked as a Mother's Help, on a temporary permit and conceived a lively distaste for the traditional British way of life – and perhaps then also for children. She would certainly have left England again, she always said, had it not been for Henry. Henry had never quite decided if, on balance, she regarded her meeting with him and marriage as a piece of unlooked-for-good-fortune (which, for a stateless person, it was) or as a regrettable curtailment of further freedom, which would only be borne with fortitude. Perhaps Livia had never quite decided herself.

In the early period of their marriage, holidays abroad had not yet become the accepted thing in Henry's circle, and, in any case, with the unsettled state of the world, Livia's paranoid fear that if she went abroad she might not be allowed back into England seemed real enough. Later, as this obsession receded and air fares came down in price, she did consent to go abroad, cloaked in the decent anonymity of her husband's passport, in the way most of their acquaintances did: package trips to Majorca or Rimini, skiing holidays in small places in Switzerland or Austria. For some reason Livia's contempt for convention in England did not extend to English-style excursions to the Continent, and she was surprisingly docile and tolerant on these routine occasions; even her emphatic Hellenism temporarily went into abeyance. But still they never went to Greece. For years she maintained she didn't want to. Then, in the mid-1960s, when package tours there began to be advertised, they talked about it inconclusively and she agreed to go – 'Though of course you realise, Henry, that it will be no holiday for *me*.' But then came the Colonels, and Livia, more Greek than ever and welcoming at their London flat a trickle of new refugees, declared that, like Melina Mercouri, she would never set foot in the land of her birth till the fascist régime was overthrown. The result was that, when the Colonels were eventually unseated, Livia behaved as if this had been the one thing all along keeping her out of her homeland and began to plan a visit there in earnest.

Henry was both elated and worried by the prospect. With some part of his mind he perceived that Livia's Greekness was acutely in need of a fresh transfusion of reality. In spite – or because – of her determination to preserve her national identity, that identity seemed in danger, as she grew imperceptibly older, of becoming a shrivelled, bloodless thing like a withered limb, more burden to her than use. But would a visit to the Greece of the present blend with Livia's memories, or would it conflict with them, destroy them? An awful lot of people seemed to be going to Greece these days. Over the years in Spain and Italy, Henry had seen the debasing effects of prosperity and the cancer of tourism at work. He knew that once-empty beaches were now lined with hotels all round the Mediterranean, and that boys who had been born in fishing villages grew up to become waiters, souvenir sellers and beach-gigolos when their villages were transformed into an aquatic suburbia. The night before they left he had a frightening dream in

79

which they had landed at Athens but it was Torremolinos. The people didn't speak Greek any more and didn't hear Livia even when she screamed at them. Livia went mad. He woke in a sweat, feeling old and exhausted, and dreading the days ahead.

But it all passed off far better than he had even hoped. They landed at Athens at dusk, and the next morning the Hertz car they had arranged to hire carried them quickly through its enormously expanded suburbs which Livia did not recognise and out to the safety of the new motor road towards the Corinthian isthmus. Henry was thankful to put Athens behind them for the moment; he had been afraid that Livia would at once insist on going in search of streets or buildings in which she had lived. He would have wanted to do that, he thought. But she didn't seem to care about this. As the days went by, and they trickled south into the Peloponnese, through inland villages blessedly unequipped for more than a handful of visitors, it gradually dawned on him that Livia hadn't come to Greece after all to confront her own past but just for Greece itself. For once her peculiar imperceptiveness of the passage of time was an advantage to her; she did not analyse or make comparisons: it was enough for her to be in her own culture.

For it was, still, her culture, he now thankfully realised. As the amazingly tranquil days succeeded one another, he marvelled to see how simply she enjoyed everything. A cup of coffee in a café was a ritual; going shopping in village shops for picnic lunches a form of joyful sacrament. For the first time he understood fully that her insistence on eating Greek food in England all these years had not, after all, been an affectation or a form of pig-headedness but something of fundamental significance, like a Jew sticking to his dietary laws in a gentile world. He felt ashamed of all the times when, temporarily exhausted by her demands, her anxieties, her arbitrary judgments and her craving for admiration, he had felt unsympathetic towards her. It had been as she had often said: he was a stuffy Britisher who did not understand temperament.

Now, as he lovingly watched her joking with waiters and shopkeepers, stopping to chat to crones sitting on front

80

doorsteps, he felt how right she had always been to stick to her own manner, her own style, even though at home it did seem unsuitably strident. He relaxed and began to enjoy himself more than he had done for years. For the first time ever in their married life he felt that – well, that here he could trust Livia not to do anything silly which would annoy people. Not that it was really like that, he told himself hastily, but that was how, in drab self-conscious England, it sometimes seemed.

Then they crossed back to the mainland to go to Delphi.

It had been, he realised before the morning was out, a mistake. For the first time that holiday Livia found herself among a horde of foreign tourists and she didn't like it at all. She didn't like the new hotels in the village of Delphi either, or the shopkeepers on the pavements inviting her to buy reproduction statuary and mass-produced bags. She walked past them, head high, occasionally saying things to them in Greek that made them fall back with a slightly stunned look on their faces. By the time they actually reached the ruins, trailing in the hot sun behind a bevy of organised Germans, she was, Henry noted with the old sick dread, in a very bad temper indeed.

He wandered round the fallen temples without seeing them, his whole being concentrated, as so often before, on sustaining Livia through her current crisis, trying to placate her but prepared, if necessary, to draw her anger upon himself rather than let her turn it toward others. By the time they reached the huge amphitheatre, as familiar as a picture of the Royal Family with their corgis, she seemed calmer, and all might yet have passed over, he thought afterwards, had it not been for the Germans.

They seemed an ill-assorted group: elderly women in linen hats and ankle socks, men in shorts carrying multiple cameras, the results of which could not possibly have justified the weight and complexity of the apparatus, sun-scorched youngsters dressed in varying degrees of unsuit-ability for the climate and the place. Livia had already, during their trip, passed various remarks on the ineptitude

81

of tourists who, despite their relative wealth, came to Greece less well equipped for hot sun and mountainous holy places than the poorest peasant. Now, in the amphitheatre, he saw her lip curl with dislike and contempt, as she surveyed sun-tops and peeling shoulders, tight jeans, wobbling high-heels and hair like dry steel wool. (She herself was, of course, dressed with impeccable suitability in soft blue cotton, flat sandals and a silk headscarf.) Henry didn't like Germans either, on the comfortable British principle that no one old enough to remember the War likes Germans, and he too wished they had not been there at that moment cluttering the amphitheatre. But why must Livia take their presence there so *personally?*

All might still have been well had it not been for the blonde German girl in the long red and blue flounced skirt: you couldn't miss her, partly because she was the most flamboyantly dressed in all that gaudily coloured troop, partly because she was, in a lacquered, trivial way, much the prettiest female there, and partly because she was showing off so much. She was jumping on and off one of the plinths that, two millennia before, had held statues of powerful and terrible deities, posing there with exaggerated gestures for other people to photograph her. Her giggles went on and on, carried by the marvellous acoustics right to where Henry and Livia sat: not intermittent laughter at this joke or that, but the continuous mindless mirth of adolescent sexual hysteria. She was one of those girls who made Henry feel glad after all that they had never had a daughter, and he muttered consolingly to Livia:

'I'd smack her bottom if she was mine and went on like that.'

'Would you indeed?' said Livia in an even, unpleasant voice. 'I expect she'd like that.'

Henry realised it had been a mistake to say anything. It was quite natural (he supposed) that Livia should be automatically critical of any young, pretty woman, but it was always difficult for him to remember that, in such circumstances, she was apt to believe the most casual and well-intentioned remark to be weighted with insulting meaning.

'She's only a kid,' he said curtly. 'She doesn't mean any harm. She's just stupid.'

'And what makes you think that *not meaning any harm* or *just being stupid* is an excuse?' asked Livia, cruelly parodying his tolerant tone. 'Most of the Nazis *didn't mean any harm* and were *just stupid* too. That's the trouble with you – you've no sensitivity or experience in these matters. And you're too lazy to think things through.'

'Oh, come on Livia . . . A silly little tourist . . .'

'A silly little *German bitch*.' She spat the words out: 'A bitch on heat. Here – in Delphi. Dirtying the most famous and holy place in the world. She is an obscenity.'

'Well, we'll wait a few minutes and I expect they'll move off,' said Henry uneasily. His soothing tone sounded priggishly inadequate in his own ears – he could never rise satisfactorily to such occasions, never match Livia's intensity of feeling. Evidently Livia thought so too, for she ground her small teeth together and cast him a look of contempt.

Perhaps it was the look that did it. Or perhaps – Henry was to reflect afterwards with a dawning self-knowledge – he himself was keyed up and elated by this visit to Delphi and actually found Livia's insane fury as hard to take in that setting as *she* found the German girl. At all events, he suddenly began getting very angry on his own account. Livia had better not push matters any further.

What Livia in fact did was get up and walk, consciously graceful, down the slope of the amphitheatre, right to the bottom where the Germans were now preparing to move off. Full of foreboding, Henry followed her. The blonde giggler was subsiding at the foot of the plinth, hanging schoolgirlishly on to the shoulders of a fat, pink companion. Henry saw clearly, from a few paces behind, as Livia walked deliberately up to her, spat at her, and then made the Greek five-fingers-outstretched sign for warding off the evil eye.

The German girl shied away, looking faintly surprised, but her vacuous face showed no hint of understanding the force of Livia's action. She and her companions did, however, moderate their shrieks to subdued titters and mutterings, and once they looked back towards Livia as the party moved off to other sites, other backcloths for photographs.

Henry caught up with Livia and grabbed her by the arm.

'Livia, what the hell did you do that for? Really you go too far –'

'*She* went too far –' replied Livia without looking at him. 'Much too far.' Her oracular, enigmatic tone enraged him further. Who the hell did she take herself for?

'She was just a visitor enjoying herself,' he said, keeping his voice steady with difficulty. 'Not in a way you or I would choose, of course – but in a way which, however silly, is essentially harmless. You've told me yourselves that the Greeks honour guests to their country – and you spit at her. You also make that sign which, you told me the other day in great detail, must never be made by accident to anyone in Greece because it puts a curse on them. Pull yourself together, Livia.'

'And just what,' she said in a small cold voice, still gazing after the departing Germans, 'do you imagine that you mean by that?'

'I mean,' he shouted violently, the patience of that hour, that day, and all the years before it, suddenly at an end. 'I mean stop behaving like a bloody, phony, self-centred, pretentious *cow*.'

In the brief anti-climax of silence that followed, she said:

'I have put a curse on her, you know. And on all of them.'

'Bloody rubbish,' said Henry violently. 'It's all just showing off with you – all of it. You may fool other Greeks but you don't fool me. Be your age, Livia!'

It was by far the hardest thing he had ever said to her and, as they began to climb one behind the other down the steep, rocky hill, he knew already that he should never have said it; that it would prove unforgivable.

At the bottom, the Germans had already been incarcerated again in a hot, mauve coach and were driven off. Livia sat in the shade and watched the coach's shiny rump disappear round the hairpin bends of the road. When she finally decided to speak to him again. Henry thought, and the storm broke from her, it would be a terrible one. Exhausted already by the events of the day and the mounting heat of the sun, he went to choose postcards at a kiosk.

He sat in the car to write them. 'Having a really marvellous holiday,' he wrote. 'Delphi is really a fascinating place. Livia sends her love.' He wrote it six times, to six different couples. Then he put the cards away in the glove compartment and started the engine. If Livia was going to sulk, then two could play at that game.

She waited till he had backed the car and turned it. Then she strolled over and got in without looking at him. Glancing sideways at her to make sure she had shut her door properly, he was surprised to find that her aquiline face wore a look of composed satisfaction. She couldn't really think she had won, could she?

They drove on into the mountains. There was a monastery somewhere up there whose frescoes they had earlier agreed they would see. Now, it was the last thing Henry felt he wanted to do; pictures secretly bored him anyway: but he felt still less able to discuss with Livia now any alternative plan.

It was a relief to give all his attention to the road, which wound up and up above sheer, unfenced drops. It was amazing, he had remarked several times already that holiday, that there weren't more terrible accidents, particularly considering the way some of the Greeks drove.

Suddenly Livia leaned forward and remarked 'There they are.' Her voice held the comfortable, unsurprised note of someone seeing reliable friends at an appointed meeting-place.

Henry looked where she was pointing, down the face of the mountain, but knew already with a sudden horrible understanding what he would see. Too neat, too crude, too violent. Too like Livia herself. The warm, sunburnt skin of his neck and shoulders grew cold and crept.

Down, far down below, stranded on its side among scrub and boulders, a broken toy on a garden rockery, lay the mauve coach. Most of its windows seemed to be smashed and above it on the mountain, as if it had bounced over and over, lay suitcases, carrier bags, cameras, shoes, bits of clothing, huddled shapes, and what might have been the torn and crumpled remnant of a long, red and blue flounced skirt.

Livia drew the comfortable sigh of one completing a good meal, then said companionably, 'We'll be at Ossios Loukas quite soon, won't we? Have you got the map handy?'

And Henry drove automatically onwards, cold and appalled within himself, towards the future.

The Dear Departed

When the black cars drew up before the semi-detached house, they were all ready and waiting. There were three cars, counting the one in front in which no one but Eric and his attendants would ride. Two others, it was felt, would be enough for the mourners. They were not a very large family, and had become dispersed with time both geographically and socially. Any friends attending the funeral would go straight to the crematorium in their own cars. After all, most people had cars these days. It wasn't like in the old days.

In the old days, all the women would have been in black, or at any rate dark grey. Eileen remembered her own mother's funeral, long ago before the War, in the little house in Deptford where they had all grown up. There had been aunts then – now forgotten dust themselves – with long black skirts, and cloaks and capes trimmed with moulting jet: lugubrious Queen Marys, they had sat in the front room all day, drinking cups of tea and talking in special black-clad voices. They would have been shocked into speechlessness to see the female descendants today. Eileen herself had not possessed a black coat for years, and was wearing her navy with a navy hat. Her sister Gladys, making a similar modern compromise, had settled for the same colour, with a blue and black patterned headscarf. Their cousin Dorothy, the one who had had a hard life, was in what she still called her 'nigger-brown costume', which Eileen thought must be a good twenty years old; and Gladys's daughter Penny was in a reddish plaid, if you please . . . Still, it was nice of her to come, Eileen told herself dully. She had cried so much over the last four days, in weariness, relief and generalised regret, that she felt completely empty, and it was almost as much of an effort to summon up decisive feelings as it was to make coherent

87

responses to people and to think about jellies and whisky. She had also, obedient to modern custom, taken several Vallium, which she found had not improved her concentration. Fortuntely Gladys and Penny were seeing to the food for afterwards, and Gladys's husband Ted was seeing to the drink. She would not, they said repeatedly, urging the tranquillisers on her, have to bother about anything.

Standing in the cramped hall pulling on her gloves (navy, too, bought yesterday) Eileen felt glad that her aunts were all dead, and many other people, too, and that it was Now and not twenty, thirty or forty years ago. She had noticed that, whereas many of her contemporaries, including her sister, idealised the past, suffering enjoyable bouts of reminiscence, she herself harboured almost the opposite of nostalgia, whatever that might be called – a degree of scorn and fear towards the past, just because it *was* the past, and over and done with. It wasn't, she considered objectively, that she had had a hard life. In certain ways (not all, of course) she had been lucky and had been spared many things. But she wouldn't wish to live it all over again, and felt impatient with those who wished they were young again or who talked about 'the good old days'. To her, long-past days, however enjoyable they had once been, were never 'good', for they exhaled too musty an odour of extinct emotions and out-of-date assumptions.

Gladys was taking her arm: it was rare that the sisters touched one another.

'You and I and George and Ruth ought to go in the first car, Ted says; and if there's room he'll come, too, or if not he'll go in the second car with Penny and the others.'

Eileen submitted docilely, for once, to Gladys's view. It didn't matter twopence anyway, did it? They were all going to the same place. George was Eric's younger brother; he had done well in business and had a big house now in Sevenoaks, which Eileen had only once visited. Ruth (his second wife) was said to be quite a nice person, but of course she was a different sort from themselves – you could tell that just by looking at her (today, a dove-grey dress with raincoat, shoes and handbag all to match). Eileen would never admit to being made shy by people like Ruth; after all, having married brothers, they were both just Mrs Simmonds, weren't they? But, as she had said several times to Eric, there was no point at all in trying to keep up with people who weren't your type, family or no family.

Wearily, Eileen let herself be installed in the car with Gladys on one side and George on the other. In the hearse ahead, the polished box like a cake with its creamy topping of flowers looked too small to contain an adult body – a phenomenon she had noticed at other funerals but always forgot in between. Of course Eric had lost a good deal of weight those last months, but it wasn't just that; the dead, no sooner expired, seemed to set themselves apart from the living, shrinking physically as well as psychologically, transforming themselves into alien entities at once both more and less than human. She had felt this when her parents died, when their brother Dick had been killed in the war, and when aunts and cousins and old acquaintances had died, but she had not expected to feel it so strongly and so immediately about her own husband.

She and Eric had been married since she was eighteen. Almost fifty years. Yet she felt as estranged from the body in the box as if it had been made of another substance than her own. She discovered to her surprise that the thought of its imminent destruction – say, in half an hour's time, or did they stock-pile bodies and burn them in batches to save fuel? – hardly touched her. *'We two shall be one flesh . . .'* But they never had been, not really, not like it seemed to suggest in the marriage service, and no children had grown from their union. Perhaps, she thought, that was why she didn't feel more at the mental picture of Eric's squat, plump frame being consumed with fire, appendix scar, in-growing toenails and all. But she had a shrewd idea that most marriages were not really the indissoluble physical union of which the prayer-book spoke. Perhaps many, many widows felt as she did, but didn't like to say so?

If she dreaded the funeral, it was for other, mundane, reasons: she was afraid of not responding to people as she ought, of not recognising some old friend of Eric's

89

afterwards or of failing to thank the clergyman at the right moment. And did close relatives enter the chapel before everyone else or afterwards? She had meant to ask Ted, but had forgotten, and now he was sitting behind her with George's Ruth. It seemed awkward to turn round, and she felt embarrassed asking such a trivial question anyway.

Ahead, the car with its decorated box went on and on through leafy avenues, past roundabouts and housing estates. Eileen tried thinking: one day it will be me in that box. It's always been other people before, but it's coming nearer. Perhaps next time it will be me. Her depression lightened a little; she felt she had perceived something, understood in a new way what a funeral was *for*. It was a rehearsal for one's own end. Eric had always hated her to say things like that; he had called her morbid, cold-blooded, unnatural, and worse. When his mother had died and she'd said it was just as well really, wasn't it, he'd thrown the dinner she'd just cooked on the floor. But then Eric had gone through life with his eyes tight shut and his ears blocked, filled with generalised fear and resentment against age, time, ill-health, change, the Council, the Government, youngsters, his brother George and – intermittently – Eileen herself.

'*I am the Resurrection and the Life, saith the Lord, and he that believeth in me . . .*' At the sudden commencement of the chaplain's voice, Eileen raised her head. She had not, till that moment, been particularly conscious of his presence. Behind her a few people were still creaking into pews. They shouldn't start, not really, till everyone was in, even if they *were* late, but that was cremation all over for you: just like a factory assembly-line. It probably wasn't the young chaplain's fault.

'*Man that is born of woman hath but a short time to live and is full of misery . . .*' Arrested in spite of herself by the force of the words, she looked at the chaplain properly for the first time.

It was Davy Lucas. Her gloved hands clutched the back of the pew in front and her heart lurched within her.

Of course, of course, she told herself as the palpitations subsided, it couldn't really be Davy. This young man could not have been born when Davy had used to call for Eric on firewatching nights at the house they lived in in Lewisham in the first years of their marriage and that was how it all began. But she stared and stared at him, slitting her eyes, seeing Davy Lucas's round dark head with its choirboy lick of hair over the forehead, Davy Lucas's large brown eyes and big mobile mouth with even white teeth, his slight build. Even this man's voice was rather like Davy's; they might have been to the same posh fee-paying school. Davy. After all these years.

'. . . *he cometh up and is cut down as a flower, he fleeth as it were a shadow and never continueth in one stay.*'

Davy had not stayed. He had, in the end, gone, quite suddenly. For three years they had known him, for half that time he and she had been lovers – and then, one day, while he and she and Eric were sitting over a scrappy meal before that night's firewatch, he had told them, just like that, that he had got himself accepted by the Army after all. Had told *them*, as a couple, so that she had to choke back her cries, her protestations. Feeling that she was indeed choking, she had got up to fetch the sweet – bottled plums, it had been and custard made with half milk and half water as you had to then.

'But what about your asthma? I thought – '

Thought you loved me too much to leave me. You said so, once. Thought we would go on in this way for ever and ever, with you and I sharing our secret world every Monday and Thursday afternoon and you and Eric firewatching at Cruft's works every Monday and Thursday evening.

'Ah, my asthma's been better the last two years. Seems the Blitz had done it good.' She looked at him then, eager to read a secret joke in his eyes, but he wasn't looking at her. 'I've been passed Grade Three,' he said.

'They only use Grade Threes for desk jobs, don't they?' she said triumphantly. 'You'll stay in London, I expect?'

'No, actually I heard today. They're sending me to Glasgow at the end of the month.'

91

So he had known about his acceptance already and had not told her. The pain of it had astonished her at the time with its intensity, and now, more than forty years later, it struck again with frightening force. Loss and betrayal swept over her like odours released from long storage, so that she felt weak and faint. In that chapel, as her husband's funeral service continued, she stood and suffered acutely, aching with new grief for a man she had hardly thought of for a life-time, eyes fixed on the stranger who was so like him.

'. . . .*And so we commit his body to the ground, earth to earth, dust to dust, ashes to ashes* . . .' As he spoke, the curtains behind the coffin parted on cue as if in a cinema and the electric organ started up; the coffin itself began to move towards the gap. It was going to disappear, with its load of expensive flowers. She tried momentarily to concentrate on it, telling herself, 'I'll never see it again' – but what was a coffin anyway? A shiny box full of nothing. Instead, she found herself repeating, in a passion of love and horror, 'I'll never see Davy again. Never. Never,' as if the full meaning of the word was something which, till that moment, she had not understood.

'Well, mind you call and see us next time you come south,' Eric had said with conscious heartiness.

'Of course I will.' Davy always spoke particularly warmly towards those he did not think much of. Still not looking at her, he went on: 'I'll miss you both – and all the delicious meals Eileen's cooked for me. You've really been good to me.'

Still unable to believe the horror that was happening to her, she followed them both to the door. For an instant, as Eric was collecting coats and tin hats, Davy's eyes and hands sought hers and she realised confusedly that he, too, was suffering, but took no comfort from this. His lips framed a sentence, something about it being 'best like this'. She tried as silently to answer him, to say, 'No,' to say, 'Wait' . . . Half a minute later he was gone.

For weeks she felt as if she had suffered some fearful physical shock. She felt, in strict truth, as if she had been bombed out – of her own body, her own feelings. In the nights she dreamed that Davy came back to her, in many different ways and guises, but in the mornings the grief and loss were there waiting for her. She confided in no one, for that was not her way. It was all very well for the other girls at the munitions' factory where she was on the early shift to regale each other with tales of love and pain, weeping on each other's shoulders when their own incidental husbands, sweethearts or fancy men were taken away: she scorned the belittling comfort of the shared emotion, of feminine complicity. In any case, if anyone had told her she would 'get over' Davy, she would have hit them. She did not want or expect to get over him. At moments she would think consciously: 'I'll never see him again.' But she did not believe it; it was as if the word 'never', like 'infinity' or 'endless', had no meaning one could really grasp.

What happened was that, as time went by, gradually the conviction that he *would* return to her one day, though not yet, solidified into a sort of principle which she accepted but no longer examined. Only by this device could she construct some sort of sides-to-middle existence out of the shreds of her happiness. It was a repair job which, as things turned out, had lasted pretty well without further examination for the next forty-odd years. Till now.

Only now, standing unhearing in the chapel as the service trundled to its close, did she understand. The past was not dead; it was not irrelevant or musty or contemptible but *real*, realer than the life she had lived in between. Her aunts were dead, her childhood was dead, her married life was dead, and Eric was dead and fast dwindling in size and significance, but what she had shared with Davy was not dead. It had never died; it had just lain dormant with its power intact, waiting till she should meet it again. *This* was love, the irreducible, unchangeable reality which, even when ignored, survived all deaths or distances.

In place of her anguished sense of a loss undiminished by the passage of years came a sense of joy that was undiminished also. What she and Davy had shared no one could take away. Even God, they said, could not undo the past. It and Davy were hers for ever.

Close to, shaking hands with people at the chapel door once the ceremony was over, the chaplain did not look so like Davy. His eyes were nearer together, she decided, and his chin was not the same. He was a bad imitation of the real thing, like margarine or leatherette. It did not matter. What mattered was what he had awakened in her own mind. She thanked him automatically for the funeral service, eyes vague and deliberately unfocused.

Wreaths were laid out on a covered veranda and people were looking at them, stooping to read the cards, covertly comparing the size of one offering with another. Eileen recognised two men from the company where Eric had worked for the last twenty years before he retired, and several people from the Rotary. She smiled at them politely, veiling contempt. Old men with red necks inside their best dark suits, hanging stomachs, bald heads, bleary eyes, obtrusively white false teeth. What had they to do with her and Davy? Inside her matronly blue coat (she had never liked herself in navy anyway, she thought) she was a slim and pretty young woman in slacks and a turban, hurrying down a known alleyway in the blackout with a string bag full of vegetables in her hand and ecstasy in her heart.

Gladys, taking charge in a flustered unaccustomed way, was inviting these people back to the house. What a bore, thought Eileen, putting her gloves in her pocket. *I* don't want to talk to them. Still, all the jelly and whisky was there and must, she supposed, be consumed. She would have liked to go quietly back home alone, and change out of these clothes and lie on her bed, just remembering.

At home, a neighbour had laid all the food out on the sideboard in the lounge, where it resembled not sustenance so much as a craft display. Jellies and what she called 'shapes' were Gladys's speciality. Crystal green dressed with angelica was flanked by chocolate, by coffee and by chocolate-coffee-pink-and-plain-white blancmange in stripes like sand layers in glass from Alum Bay. Alongside, slices of candied lemon and orange hung in gelatine suspension as if in amber. The hard glossy surfaces, piped with rigid whipped cream, made it look inedible, but at least it gave people something to talk about to get them going. Penny began plying them with plates of sandwiches (her contribution) with the abashed air of one half-apologising for their crude unpretentious reality.

Tea was made, in a large number of borrowed pots that seemed to empty too quickly. Eileen wondered when it would be considered right to start on something stronger. She and Eric always liked a drink. She knew that, if she drew Ted aside to the kitchen and asked him, he would at once press a double on her and stand there while she drank it discreetly, like medicine. But she was sick of people like Ted and Gladys making a fuss of her. She would rather wait, politely, like a guest in her own house.

She made efforts to move about the crowded room, smiling at people and accepting sandwiches, which she then abandoned.

'. . . . Such a nice service, I thought. Didn't you think it was a nice service, Eileen? . . . Oh, she didn't hear me . . .'

'. . . I thought he spoke very nicely, didn't you, Dot? Very sincere.'

'. . . rather *young*, but still . . .'

'. . . Not at all like the one we got for Mother, and that only cost nine pounds. 'Course, that was two years ago now.'

'. . . More tea?'

'. . . No, I won't have another ham one, thanks. Tell you what, though, is that some fish paste young Penny's got there? I wouldn't mind . . .'

'. . . No, they're with their auntie for the afternoon. I mean, they're too young . . .'

'. . . White as a sheet. So I said, "Whatever's the matter, Glad?" And she said, "That was Eileen on the phone. Eric's passed on." Quite upset, she was, it being sudden. Mind you, we were all expecting it, you might say, but it's different when it happens, isn't it?'

95

'. . . Sure? I can easily fetch some more hot water.'

'. . . taking it?'

'Oh, very well really, very well. But, then, she always had a lot of self-control, Eileen. She's like *her* mother in that.'

'. . . and we used to go for cycle rides. When the children were young. Really nice, that was – lovely down that way. We used to take a picnic and that. It's all been built over now.'

'. . . Thirty thousand. Yes. Of course it would be quite a bit more now.'

'. . . they'd forgotten all about the dog! So the postman said . . .'

'Thanks. I wouldn't say no . . .'

Finding a small oasis of space near the window, Eileen revolved in it, hands empty, trying to look contented and occupied. Presently she realised that a man was standing near her, also apparently alone. One of those fat, bald, red-faced men like all the rest of them. He said, 'I don't suppose you remember me.'

'Oh, yes, I do,' she lied easily. He was sure to be a Rotarian or someone from the bowling club or one of the regulars from the Crown; she would find out which if he went on talking. But in fact there *was* something familiar about him, particularly his voice, though he was wheezing and coughing as he spoke. She waited without interest for further enlightenment.

'Did Eric tell you he'd run into me again, then? . . . Ah, I thought not. Last December, that would have been.'

'Oh, yes?' she said, computing the months. 'That would have been just before – just before his illness.'

'Yes. He did tell me actually that he was going into hospital soon to have his – er – trouble looked at. But he didn't seem to think then that it was anything serious.' He hesitated, wheezing, then said, 'I'm very sorry, Eileen.'

'Oh,' she said, confused and puzzled that this stranger had called her by her christian name. 'Oh, well – yes. Thank you. But, after all, we all have to go sometime. That's what I tell myself.'

'Too true,' he said lugubriously, 'Too true . . . I haven't been well myself recently.'

'Oh, I'm sorry,' she said automatically.

'No. Chronic bronchitis. At least, that's what they call it.' He coughed for a long time as if in demonstration. She recoiled from him a little. 'Asthma,' he said at last. 'They say you never really get over it, don't they?'

She said boldly, 'Where *did* you run into Eric . . . Run into him again, I mean?'

'It was at Charing Cross,' he said 'I was just on my way to see my daughter. She's married now – lives in Dartford . . . My wife died two years ago . . . But perhaps you didn't know I was married?'

'I don't believe I did,' she said, feeling baffled and socially at sea. Perhaps she should have had something to eat after all – or perhaps she shouldn't have taken those Vallium pills. That was Gladys's fault.

'1945,' he said. 'My wife was from Edinburgh. When I was demobbed I worked in insurance there. But the climate never really suited me. I got transferred to the head office and we moved south when my daughter was five. We lived in Hendon. I mean, I still do.'

She thought: Why are you telling me all this? I'm not a bit interested in you. But she said, feeling that some degree of effusiveness must be called for, 'It must be lonely for you now your wife's dead.'

'Too right,' he said, coughing, 'too right.' She looked at his heavy hangdog face and tried to imagine him as a younger man, casting vaguely about in her memory for clues, but the impression he gave of age, debility and repectable, undefined failure blotted out everything else. He seemed, she thought, tiresomely self-absorbed. That was the loneliness, probably.

'Actually,' he was going on doggedly, 'it's pure coincidence that I heard poor old Eric was dead. I mean, Hendon's the far side of London.'

She agreed, helplessly.

'I'll tell you how it was,' he went on determinedly. 'As I said, when I ran into Eric at Charing Cross I was going to see my daughter. Well, when I got there I told her about it – about how I'd run into an old friend from the war, and how

I'd recognised him at once because he'd hardly changed a scrap, but he didn't recognise me at first. You know,' he said in a burst of desperate confidence, 'I was glad to have something interesting to tell me daughter. I mean, you try to think up things to interest them, but it isn't always easy, is it?'

'I don't know,' she said abstractedly. 'We never had any, you know.' Who? *Who?*

'Well anyway,' he said in a rush, as if already regretting his confidence. 'I told my daughter about him. And, of course, as she lives down this way, too, she has the same local paper as you. And last week she happened to glance at the deaths column, though I'm sure she doesn't usually, and she saw about Eric. And she remembered the name from my telling her and sent the cutting to me. And that's how I came to be here.'

'So that's how,' she said faintly. Awareness was just beginning to dawn. She felt incredulous to the point of scorn, yet with every second the belief was growing.

'I bet you're surprised to see me,' he said, with a flicker of his old, debonair manner, which was followed at once by a fit of coughing.

'Oh, no,' she said at random, 'That is – for the first minute I didn't – I didn't recognise you, but now – ' Wildly ticking off points in her mind. Dark hair? He'd lost it, of course – had already been losing it actually, when she had known him; that was why he had brushed it forward in that way – and what he hadn't lost was quite grey. Eyes? Dulled and sunken. Mouth? Sunken, too. Unlike most men his age, he seemed to have rather too few teeth in his mouth instead of too many. She thought that on balance a gleaming plate would have been better. Figure? Lost. Voice?

Yes. She should have remembered his voice. Voices last, after all, when bodies have turned to flab and wasted muscle, when youth and energy and health are all spent. But his voice – though now at last she had recognised it clearly – was much altered. Between youth and age it had changed in timbre; it had been overlaid with the intonation of nearly thirty years in the company of a Scottish wife;

above all, it was distorted by his continual wheezing and coughing. Asthma, indeed. His lungs must be rotting away. Perhaps that was partly why he seemed so dreary, so spent, so *old*. He couldn't be much more than Eric's age and yet he seemed a broken old man. Compared with him, she felt young, brisk, well organised. What on earth had brought him here this afternoon? A desire to rehearse his own imminent ending? What a cheek. What a nerve – just turning up like this. How dare he come back in this way, uninvited? Did he think that after forty-odd years she was going to fall on his neck and beg him to come and live with her?

Her strongest desire was to turn and leave him, old, red-faced, coughing and boring as he was. He was disgusting, too, now that she looked at him more closely; not really respectable at all. His shirt wasn't clean, and there were food stains on his tie. Of course, he never had been a tidy dresser. *And always a bit of a sponger*, her mind whispered to her.

She wanted to go right away from him, away to her own room and shut out the irrelevant present. She wanted to lie on her bed with her shoes off and slip away effortlessly into the past. There, Davy Lucas would come to her, untouched by time, unchanged and unchanging. There, she would be loved for ever; he would have no faults, and all time would be one. She yearned, like a new addict, for her room, for the quilted silk bedcover beneath her stockinged feet, for peace and nothingness and ecstasy. For the Resurrection and the Life that lay within herself and nowhere else at all.

Fuoripista

Standing on skis beside the Italian instructor, waiting in the queue for the chair-lift, William suddenly asked:

'What does *fuoripista* mean?'

'*Fuoripista?*' The flowery word sounded more convincing on Bruno's lips. 'It means,' he said, ' "Outside-of-the-piste", like we say. "Off-piste" isn't it? To ski not where there is usual place but down another way. Is dangerous for people who do not know.'

'Oh, I see. I see. I saw in an Italian newspaper that those people who were killed above Courmayer the other week were skiing *fuoripista.*' He did not add that he had first supposed it meant something like a carnival.

'Yes. Four Italians, isn't it, and some English too, I think? I read also. The men of the chair-lift, they say, "No, that way is dangerous now in the spring. The snow can slip." But the skiers, they think they know best – and see, this happen.'

'Silly fools.'

'Is very sad. People with not enough experience, they do not realise.' Bruno was a sanguine and forgiving young man, useful attributes, William thought, in an instructor taking an elementary class. If he himself had been an instructor, he thought, he would have been driven to exasperation days ago by the mixture of incompetents, semi-incompetents (his actual category) and foolhardy teenage beginners, which constituted the week's group. But presumably, to be an effective instructor, you must simply like people, as well as snow and mountains. He felt humble and admiring. The pretty, clumsy young secretaries in the class might, he supposed, be falling in love with Bruno in the time-honoured way for his physical ability, but it was rather the young man's tolerant geniality that he, William, felt he would never learn to emulate.

And yet none of his acquaintances and neither of his two old friends would have called him an intolerant man. He was mild-mannered, even anxiously polite at times, and had been so since his heavily-regulated only-childhood. His temper, with the exception of rare outbursts at his school-boy sons about bubble-gum or rudeness at table, was kept far under control, somewhere in the inaccessible depths of his being. In his professional life as a solicitor specialising in family trusts, his role was to support, to comprehend, to restrain, to place emotion-charged matters on a practical, manageable footing. And in his personal life also this had been for years his role; not so much now with the boys, who were getting bigger and more self-sufficient, but increasingly with Rosemary, his wife.

Long ago (it seemed to him now) Rosemary had not needed his support and understanding so much. Long, long ago, in that childhood to which she was still, in her forties, nostalgically attached, she had apparently been brave and happy and successful. She had, according to her own account, liked her boarding school, ridden ponies in the holidays, even gone sailing on the Norfolk Broads and on the Isle of Wight with Tom, her exacting and charismatic father. (She too had been an only child.) Those antique, sunlit holidays seemed to have become for her, in adult life, a high-water mark of pleasure, a standard against which all else was measured, a vision poignantly pursued across the wet, gritty Augusts of the boys' childhood. Indeed, for a number of years she had insisted on family holidays in either Norfolk or the Isle of Wight as if these locations were a foregone conclusion which did not even require discussion – until he had nerved himself to point out, somewhat forcibly (they had all suffered from concealed boredom and a sense of being out of place) that since none of them, including Rosemary herself, actually *liked* sailing for its own sake, or displayed any aptitude for it, it might be better if the following year they went to Spain or Italy instead. The boys were turning into good swimmers, and he himself felt the need of proper sunshine, not to mention cheap wine, for at least one fortnight a year . . .

102

They had gone to Majorca, and it was there, so far off the narrow course of her ordinary life, that Rosemary had begun to show the signs of what became later to be referred to as her 'first breakdown'. But that, he had tried to convince himself and her, was just fortuitous, or at the most Majorca had been a mere precipitating factor. Surely what was more relevant was that charismatic Tom, exacting to the last, had died of cancer the preceding winter, and seemed to have taken away with him some vital, unnameable ingredient from his daughter's personality.

It was a pity Tom had not been a skier rather than a yachtsman. If only he had been, and Rosemary's childhood memories had been of Swiss resorts and old-fashioned wooden skis, how differently she might have felt now about the 'glaring light of the snow' which gave her such headaches, and about 'all these boring people going on about turns'. Even the physical unfitness and timidity which prevented her from wanting to learn to ski herself might not have mattered had her intellectual distaste for the sport been transformed by memories of her father, heroic against the blue Alpine sky. The sight of her husband and sons in such postures did not, it seemed, have the same effect on her, as he had once hoped it might. Instead, she stayed inside the hotel most of the time, reading a weighty biography of Shelley's first wife who had committed suicide in the Serpentine, it seemed, and being irritable when William and the boys, glowing from the ski-slopes, came back late for lunch.

'I thought we'd agreed on one o'clock . . .'

'But Mum, it's not our fault, there was a huge queue for the shuttle-bus down from Santa Anna. James and me did the top run there today, and Phillipo said –'

'Darling, really, does it *matter* if we have lunch at one or at one thirty? We are on holiday . . . Anyway, what will you drink, now we are here?'

'I've had my drink already. I had it nearly an hour ago, as a matter of fact. You see, you did say you would be here before.'

Her one drink. And if he said, 'Well, have another now?'

she would look at him with pained reproach. She was frightened of becoming an alcoholic, and perhaps she was right: he had never quite decided how genuine was the risk of her drinking too much, at home in all those hours when he was at work and the boys away at school. It might well be, as she said, that she was tempted to drink to excess on her own – but might it not also be that her fear of this was in itself pathological, just another piece of the straight-jacket of anxieties and prohibitions with which, increasingly over recent years, she had surrounded herself?

It was maddening to come down from an exhilarating morning on the slopes and be met by this self-pitying reader of important literature, hunched inside her matronly fur coat, acidly contemplating her solitary, long-digested 'one drink'. '. . . *It is my one indulgence, Willam*' (pathetically) – '*You do think I'm right to have it, don't you?*' '*Good lord, yes, darling. I think you've been awfully sensible about this.*' She needed badly to be told she was being sensible. It was these little services that only he could perform for her which kept her going these days.

Of course she herself, not skiing, was not 'on holiday' in any real sense of the term: it was unrealistic and selfish of them (he told himself) to expect her to be enjoying herself here, for how could she? Next year, James had remarked the other evening with apparent ingenuousness, wouldn't it be more sensible to leave Mummy at home, since there didn't seem to be much for her to do here? But William, steeped in experience of Rosemary's mental patterns, could imagine only too well, and dreaded, the crisis that might be lying in wait on their return were they ever to attempt such a 'sensible', realistic step. And in a few years time, when the boys were grown up, it would presumably be even harder for him ever to leave Rosemary on her own. Blank vistas of the future assaulted him. As if confronted physically by a glaring whiteness, he shut his eyes – and then opened them again quickly.

He and Bruno had almost reached the head of the queue. He transferred his sticks to one hand and grasped them tightly, nerving himself for the hasty, ski-hampered scramble into the moving chair, an art he had not yet perfected.

The subsequent moment of relief when the chair swung out clear into the pure, empty air above the mountain was, by contrast, a surcease of exquisite peace, an interlude of suspension in every sense in which, each time, William realised just how tense and effortbound his activity on the ground had been. The lift moved soundlessly upwards; snow, fir trees and inaccessible precipices sailed beneath them as in a dream of skiing rather than the reality.

'OK this time?' Bruno asked kindly. Yesterday, William had had trouble getting his skis over the foot-rest and one of them had nearly come off.

'Yes, fine. Just fine. You know, I always hope,' he said suddenly, 'that dying will be like this.'

Bruno gaped at him. Perhaps he had not understood – 'dying' not presumably being a useful word in the multi-lingual vocabulary of a ski instructor, in spite of his remarks about skiing off-piste – or perhaps he simply could not believe his ears. William reminded himself that these god-like young men were, after all, very ordinary local boys apart from their special skill: Bruno had told him, in answer to a question, that he worked as a house-painter during the summer. William had tried to discuss with Rosemary how strange it must be to have two quite separate identities, hoping to interest her in the psychological aspect of the situation, but she had said that if he said another word about skiing she would go mad: it was bad enough James and Thomas talking of nothing else – 'but really, William, I wish you'd be your age, at least.'

He had wanted to shout, 'I am being my age. I am forty-four and not particularly fit: it is hard learning to ski at my age, and I'm not doing badly at all, and of course I'm pleased about it and want you to be pleased for me. Hell, is that so much to ask?'

But of course he did not, because he never said things like that to Rosemary these days; the equality between them which would once have made such frank and selfish expressions of personal feeling on his part possible had,

105

somewhere along the line, gone. And if ever James or Thomas gave any intimation of thinking that 'Mum's problems' were anything other than her undeserved misfortune (which had happened once or twice recently, rather worryingly) he was quick to slap down on this lack of consideration. A nervous breakdown, he briskly repeated to them once again, was no more the 'fault' of the sufferer than a broken ankle or an attack of 'flu: they were, he told them sternly, quite old enough to understand that.

'But 'flu and things get better,' Thomas had said astutely once, eyeing his father to see how the daring remark would be taken. James, older, avoided William's gaze, but he had at times an expression on his face – hard, scornful – that William did not like. Sometimes, over the last few years, he had consoled himself with the thought that the boys, at least, were not suffering crucially from Rosemary's retreat into a world of self-absorbed neurosis. They had each other, and their school life, and all their hobbies, and he himself did his best, with ploys like skiing holidays, to make life good for them. He had even dared to hope that Rosemary's long-drawn-out 'illness' might be beneficial to them, in the long run, in teaching them compassion and forbearance. But it had occurred to him recently that if you expected too much of these commodities in children, you might in fact stunt and impede sympathy's natural growth, as a muscle overstrained before it is ready is permanently weakened rather than strengthened by the experience. He tried to shut his mind to this possibility. You could not, he thought helplessly, worry about everything.

Thank heavens that Rosemary had disdained, with a shudder, the boys' casual suggestion that she herself should take a ride up in the chair-lift just to see what it was like – 'You ought to try it, Mum. It's a super view.' They could not know – he did not intend that they should know, at their age – that their mother had made a number of suicide threats and one semi-serious attempt, and that a morbid attraction-cum-fear regarding heights was part of her syndrome. He had been relieved to find (such was the perpetual, habitual undercurrent to his days) that their

106

hotel bedroom here did not have a balcony. This constant vigil, this strained watch over circumstances, chance, his own tongue, he now took for granted.

An hour or so later, as he zig-zagged his way, tense and perilous but triumphant, down the last slope again towards the bottom lift-station, Bruno said to him:

'Is better, William, eh? *Pas mal du tout! Va bene!* This afternoon, I think, you don't need me to come here with you.'

'Do you really think so?' said William, absurdly elated. 'Of course I'd love to come and practise on my own – it's marvellous up here, the snow's so good and the air's so clear. But I don't feel I really know the run yet, and I'm a bit afraid of wandering on to the wrong piste – the one the experts use.'

'No – why? Is easy!' said Bruno, distractedly casting an eye around his class. 'You just keep the lift on the right all the time. The drag-lift I mean, not the chairs – Ay-oh! Pam, what happen to you, you fall again? *Ah, là, là* John, the stick of mountain *before*, I say, always before. Is not possible to ski unless!'

Pam was the class rabbit (a rôle William was gratified not to find himself filling): she was a lacrymose-looking girl from Nottingham whose nose reddened more and more in the mountain sun. She had come skiing with her friend, who was prettier, happier and more athletic. Pam, alone of the class, looked as if she were resenting and regretting the whole enterprise. With his sensitivity morbidly sharpened to women like Pam, William could imagine all too clearly how, in another ten years, without some unexpected piece of luck, her amorphous dissatisfaction with life would have hardened into a throttling negativism, a carapace of unadjusted, unexpressed resentment that would destroy her . . . But at least Pam, un-pretty and unmarried at – what? twenty-seven? – and likely to remain so, would have some excuse for depression, whereas Rosemary, with her well-established husband, attractive home, thriving sons . . . his mind slid, against his wish, into its accustomed, obsessive track. Well, what else *did* she want?

107

What else did she expect, she who had had to make few efforts either to attain or to retain these prizes for which many women yearned in vain? A job, perhaps – a career even, which women seemed to want so much these days? But she had never said so, or indeed made the slightest move in such a direction. Even his hopeful suggestion, last year, that she might enjoy reading for a degree with the Open University, had been received without enthusiasm. Did he really expect her – her with her sleeping problems – to get up at six in the morning to watch television programmes, she had enquired? He obviously had no conception what it was *like* for her.

No, he thought wearily, perhaps he hadn't. Finally all rational arguments foundered against that. 'She has many unmet needs,' a psychiatrist she had been seeing a couple of years back had confided to him in an oracular manner. The common-sense rejoinder was, 'Dammit, haven't we all? Haven't I? This is surely the nature of the human condition. Why should she be so exclusive in her refusal to face the facts?' But he had long learnt that such an approach was unacceptable, or useless anyway, which came to the same thing. Lesson One was that, in dealing with a depressive, you simply did not commit the sin of *lèse-dépression*. Depression was like religious faith or ecstasy: you could not ever question its basis without putting yourself irrevocably in the wrong; in fact merely to be the one who was undepressed (however sympathetic) was to carry some faint stigma of insensitivity, or at any rate a touch of coarse-grained ordinariness. Rosemary was special and different: that much had always been understood long ago, when she was not a tense, over-weight woman in a fur coat but was Tom's smiling, slender, delicate daughter with whom no young man was going to be allowed to take liberties. It was almost as if, since she couldn't after all be different from other people in one way, by being beautiful or gifted or distinguished, she was going to be so in another, whatever the cost to herself or others . . .

As if fleeing in dread from the conclusion to which his thoughts had carried him, William shuffled his skis hastily down into a snow-plough, and slushed luxuriantly down the last fifty yards to the bottom of the slope.

Over lunch that day he nagged the boys, noisy and exuberant as ever after their own lesson, into promising that that afternoon they would stay going up and down on the drag-lift and practising their parallel turns, and not go off together unaccompanied to try anything new. They were both becoming proficient skiers, but probably not as proficient as they believed themselves to be, and he dreaded the accident that might befall such a pair on a strange slope. Suppose they were to wander off-piste, carelessly chattering and fooling, showing off to one another, oblivious of the dangers that lurked on almost any mountain . . . Skiing was so inherently unsafe, he thought, or rather unsafe-guarded: it was a matter of perpetual judgment, constant vigil, with the line between sunlit fun and mortal peril so very thin. That, possibly, was part of its peculiar charm and excitement. And, as Bruno had said, the snows were softened by the afternoon in the spring sunshine. If James or Thomas should, by mistake, reach a threateningly steep cul de sac and, panicking in the soft icing-sugar, slither helpless over some precipitous bluff . . .

His mind winced away from such horror, and he dragged it back into more familiar and permissable channels. As a chronic worrier, a compulsive envisager and dreader, he had learnt years ago that beyond a certain pitch of conscientiousness life became intolerable both for himself and for those dear to him; in certain circumstances discipline and common sense lay in *not* imagining and trying to forestall every conceivable eventuality. He must not let the boys grow up timid and over-instructed as he himself had done; rather than weighting them with pro-hibitions he must boost their own self-reliance and judge-ment. Such had been his principle for years, and he flattered himself now that it had worked. All the same – he made them promise, each in turn, to stay on the nursery slopes that afternoon. Both promised, though James seemed resentful.

James worried him a little, at times. Though he was the

109

elder, and very able at school, he was on the whole less reliable than Thomas, and lately with adolescence looming, William thought he had sometimes detected in James an unpleasant hint of a new and adult recklessness. He felt his imagination slither again towards a dangerous brink, seeing James in a few years time, driving unsafe cars too fast, experimenting wantonly with alcohol and drugs and whatever other horrors the young had discovered by then: James mutilated, James dead, James reduced to a vegetable – He pulled his mind up short. That way madness lay. Cope with every day, every situation as it came. That was the only way. He had learnt that by now, at least in theory. He had lived so long with a perpetual background of dread, a foreboding that remained constant but took different shapes of horror – James or Thomas bloodstained, drowned, gone for ever; Rosemary dangling from the top of the loft ladder, Rosemary with an empty pill bottle beside her, Rosemary lying with a broken neck in the hotel forecourt – that it sometimes seemed to him, in his more ironic moments, that at least there was nothing, really nothing now, that Fate could hope to spring on him unexpectedly. If nothing else, he was forearmed.

It had surprised him a little this holiday that Rosemary, who was made so anxious by so many things, did not seem to worry at all about the boys out on the ski-runs. But perhaps that was because, with no experience of skiing herself, she did not grasp the dangers. Although she tended to treat the boys as if they were still six and seven, her fears for them ran only in known and narrow tracks. Thus she was still anxious about their crossing roads, and distressed if they had colds or temperatures, but she had never seemed to give a thought to the possibility of one of them drowning in a boating accident, in the days of windy sojourns in Norfolk. Water, evidently, was sanctified and rendered harmless by Tom's memory. Snow offered no menace because it was outside her ken.

He managed the chair-lift alone that afternoon without mishap, and again enjoyed that extraordinary respite from tension, from life itself, as he was swung out alone across the white void. It seemed to him, however, that the experience was less exhilarating than it had been that morning, the light less intense, and presently he realised this was not a mere trick of the mind. A mass of clouds had moved up behind the nearer mountains, and the further range, tipped by Monte Rosa, was no longer visible. The sun was a milky haze. When he left the lift-station at the top of the piste a tiny flurry of miniature snowflakes stung his cheeks.

'Blowing up cold,' said an elderly but aggressively fit Scot whom he had met before on this slope.

William almost welcomed it. He sweated a lot, making his daring and uncertain way down the pistes which more experienced skiers managed with ease; and anyway the brilliant blue-and-white of a sunlit snowscape seemed to him too like a holiday postcard to be real: lovely of course but disconcertingly vulgar. Snowy mountains *should* be cold.

'Mustn't waste time,' said the Scot, adjusting his efficient rucksack. William nodded, but without understanding the import of the words, supposing the man was being brisk merely because such was his nature.

The Scot disappeared down the first slope. William followed more slowly, falling down once – had the snow got a little icier since this morning, or had he himself stiffened over lunch? – and by the time he reached the first of the gentle, wide-open pistes he had lost sight of the man. For a moment he felt uncertain and alone. But this was silly, he knew the way, had been down twice with Bruno and the class – and anyway there were other skiers there in the distance. He made an effort to lessen the space between himself and them.

It seemed colder coming down than it had on top, and was certainly snowing now: not much, but persistently, a fine white powder blowing across his goggles, scraping his cheeks and lips. He felt glad of his good quality down mitts, and hoped that the boys had worn jerseys under their anoraks. Not that, on the nursery slopes, they were far from the hotel, whereas here . . .

111

He enjoyed himself for a few minutes, practising leisurely turns with no one to tell him his shoulders or his sticks were at the wrong angle. But then, on the next steep bit, he fell again, rather heavily, bumping his hip and jarring his wholy body. He lay there crossly, knowing it had been his own fault, that he had swung his weight the wrong way at the crucial moment just as Bruno had often said he did.

His left ski had become detached, and was held only by the safety binding. He had a struggle, there on the slope, to get everything done up again, and had to take his mitts off to do it: by the time he put them on again his hands were numb and he let one of his sticks slip down to the bottom of the slope. Feeling craven, and glad no one was watching him, he shuffled down on his bottom to retrieve it, treating the skis as if they had been a sledge.

When he stood up again, carefully edging his skis against a further sudden descent, he realised that he had not come down exactly where the class had this morning. At least, it seemed to him not. It was hard to tell: in this fine, blowing whiteness that, like smoke, obscured the clear line between snow and sky, the landscape looked different. But it was all right, he told himself firmly as if speaking to one of the boys; there was no need to worry. All he had to do was to follow Bruno's direction, given that morning, to keep to the right of the lift – the small drag-lift that was separate from the chair-installation. He could still see that clearly.

He continued, slowly and with care, remembering at each turn to swing his weight the right way, confident that at any minute he would reach another chain of clearly-remembered, wide, easy slopes leading to the final, slightly steeper descent. But he did not reach them, and his confidence began to subside.

The next slope was harder, not easier, and there were rocks. He did not remember rocks.

He caught sight of a man, possibly the Scotsman again, skiing not far below him but on another slope. How the hell had the man got there? There didn't seem any connecting channel between that lower piste and his own.

Bruno had said 'Keep to the right of the lift.' Hadn't he? Or had he said – or meant – 'Keep the lift on your right?' In any case he couldn't see the drag-lift now. Perhaps he was already down below its level. He could see the chair-lift, indeed he was not far from it. There was nobody on it and the chairs were stationary. Had it been stopped because the weather was deteriorating?

He did not remember skiing before down any piste that ran as near to the chair-lift as this. And indeed what he recalled seeing from the lift was, at least in part, unscalable heights broken by precipices.

But he was all right, he told himself, attempting to wipe the flying whiteness away from his goggles. He was sensible and cautious and alert to dangers and did not take risks – the main thing was to get down to the intermediary lift-station now as quickly as possible.

He was still telling himself that, in a desperate incantation, three turns later, when he landed awkwardly on some ridged and freezing snow, slipped hard and then began to roll.

Shocked into a horrified realization of the place to which he had come, he flung out an arm, dropping his stick but grabbing hold of a passing boulder. For an instant, he believed he had retrieved himself from the brink. But he could not hold on. The icy rock rasped itself out from under his desperate, useless mitt-padded fingers, and he was projected head-first, backwards, away from it.

Then, like a blinding flash of blue-and-white across his eyes, like the revelation of an inner void of dazzling emptiness, a consummation of everything that, in his inmost being, he had ever dreaded – he knew. It was not Rosemary, or James or Thomas who were on the edge of extinction: it was himself. He who had held everything together, who had with unceasing effort kept the whole show of family life on the road, who had chivvied and exhorted the boys, had supported Rosemary by sharing her narrow prison, he who had prided himself on sticking to the path of duty – he was slithering and rolling uncontrollably downwards, sticks lost, skis crossed and twisting, body

113

battered, going faster and faster towards the cataclysmic edge, towards the annihilation which he had perhaps, unknowingly, been seeking for himself all the time, all those aching years, to smash at last without further warning into the white void –

Fuoripista.

An Independent Woman

When Nalini and I were at school together, she was always the one who wanted to do things. I was a dreadful stick-in-the-mud, she used to say. How would I ever get on in life if I was so afraid of everything and worried so about everything? 'It isn't *natural!*' she used to tell me.

That made me worry because *she* fussed so. Left to myself I didn't think I did too badly. I knew I was a bit feeble; my handwriting was (and is) too neat, and I always got my homework done in good time. Also, I used to button up my gaberdine mac and wear my school scarf in winter because I just didn't like being cold. But there are worse things, I sometimes thought crossly to myself, than being feeble. Anyway, if I hadn't been careful about things it would have worried Mum, who had enough worries what with Daddy being dead and her arthritis and all the things she read in the newspapers. Nalini never seemed to understand that I really didn't want to upset Mum. Nalini's own parents weren't a bit like that: I supposed she reckoned they could look after themselves. (They kept a pub.) As I say, I didn't entirely think that Nalini was right, but when you're a kid you don't know quite what to think and she got me all bothered. After she'd been having one of her goes at me I *was* afraid – afraid that she knew something about the world which I didn't; afraid that, like she said, I'd never be any use for anything and never get anywhere and that no one would ever want to marry me. We thought a lot about marriage in the fifth year at the High School; even Nalini did. I suppose that Women's Lib had come in by then to places like London and Brighton but it hadn't reached Towminster. I'm not sure it has yet.

Of course she wasn't called Nalini then. Her name was Susan. But that was far too ordinary so she called herself Julie, and even made most of the teachers call her that too.

Later, when she was in London, she became Francesca for a while . . . But I'm jumping ahead. Anyway, I call her Nalini because that's what she is now, and it does in a way suit her.

It may seem odd that she actually got the teachers to call her by a name she'd chosen, but Susan-Julie-Nalini was like that: she impressed people, even grown ups, and made them believe in her. She was good at things: not so much at Maths or Biology or French, but good at English and Art and Music, and very good at acting: she took the lead several years running in the school play. She never got very good marks in exams, and actually only passed a couple of O levels which I believe shook even her, but the staff all thought it was because she didn't take work seriously. If only she'd tried she might have been brilliant, they suggested. But Nalini didn't really seem to want to test the theory. At any rate, after O levels she wouldn't re-take any of them, or stay on to do A levels, though earlier she had talked of university. She couldn't think, she said, how people could be so unadventurous as to stay on at dreary old school doing irrelevant things when they could be out in the world getting experience. And anyway, she said, men didn't like brainy women: if I wasn't very careful I'd find that I was scaring all the boys off, with my eight O levels and however many silly A levels it was that I was planning.

I became afraid inside myself that Nalini might be right, because I thought that someone who so airily used words like 'relevant' surely knew what she was talking about. But I didn't really see that I had an alternative to work, not being pretty myself, or brilliant, let alone good at Art and Music. I wasn't all that sure anyone would ever marry me anyway, so I thought I might at least go to college and then perhaps I might get a better job later on, which would be some consolation.

Jobs were easy to get in those days, even in Towminster. Nalini got one right away, as a receptionist in a house agents. That winter she was always wanting me to go out with her – to the cinema, or to the new discotheque where the old Rainbow Ballroom had been, or just to sit in

116

the High Street coffee bar or in the Kings Arms – the 'in' pub where the sixth form boys from the Grammar School and the students from the Polytechnic used to drink. Of course, coming from a pub herself, Nalini thought nothing of sweeping in and sitting in the lounge bar with another girl. But I don't think even she would have been quite comfortable doing that on her own, which I suppose is why she wanted me to come along. As I wasn't earning and she was, she often used to pay for me, which was nice of her. One thing I will say for Nalini, she's always been generous – with money and presents, I mean. Often I didn't much want to come. I was doing three A levels, English, History and French, which is quite a lot actually, particularly if you haven't got anyone in your family who can help you or explain things to you. (Mum was very keen on my studying, but she'd never done much in that line herself.) I had a lot of reading to do, but fortunately the more I did the more I found I enjoyed it. Really, I wanted to stay in and read or write essays most evenings more than I wanted to traipse around in the cold hoping to talk to boys. But it seemed mean to say no to Nalini; she obviously needed someone like me around. She acted very jolly, but I could see she was bored and a bit lonely. Her job wasn't using her talents. An idiot could have done it, I thought: it didn't seem all that 'relevant'.

Of course, being Nalini, she didn't stay in that job. No stick-in-the-mud, her. Before the spring she'd got herself something much more to her liking, on the front desk of the new Holiday Inn out on the Birmingham Road. It still seemed to me, the odd time I went there, that there wasn't much to *do* in the job, just an awful lot of sitting round looking vaguely bright and pleasant, but Nalini enjoyed the atmosphere – the thick carpets and the people coming and going. Quite soon she had a boyfriend (one of the waiters, an Italian) and then – after some scenes I heard quite a lot about – a different one, a commercial traveller who often stayed in the hotel on business.

Well, you know what they say about commercial travellers. When I said that to Nalini, she said, What did I take

117

her for? She was nobody's fool, she said; she knew exactly what she was about. And anyway Bruce wasn't like that. Well, I don't know if he was or not. I know that Nalini got desperately worried one time because her period was late . . . At least, I *think* that was what was worrying her. But perhaps I misunderstood. And anyway she did manage to survive Bruce, one way or another, because the next thing was that she had a new friend and he was a young trainee manager. Which was one-up to Nalini.

I would have supposed that, with all this going on in her life, Nalini wouldn't have much time to spare for me any longer. But in fact she seemed to want me around as much as ever, to talk to and to try out her new ideas. With each boyfriend she changed a bit – different clothes, different manner, a few new words. When she was with Mario she had adopted a very faint foreign accent, with Bruce it was talk about money (which had never seemed to interest her much before). Now she was with this trainee manager she began to speak as if she too saw the hotel business as a serious career, rather than just a way of filling in time till marriage. I came to the conclusion that it must be rather tiring for her changing her personality so often: she probably needed me there as someone who knew what she was really like and who was always the same.

I used to know when a relationship was on its way out with Nalini because she would start hectoring me again about wasting my life. When she was happy she wanted to share her happiness with me, inviting me to drinks or even meals with her current fellow. When she was unhappy she would never admit it, but she would start having a go at me about my hair or my skirt length, or how I ought to see the world and did I mean to stay an old maid for ever? She meant it for the best, I expect, but it did get on my nerves sometimes.

After the trainee manager (Nalini said he had become 'snobbish' and 'bad tempered', but I think the firm just moved him on elsewhere) there was Peter, who used to drink in the Holiday Inn bar and whom even her parents, who weren't fussy, thought was much too old for her. Then

– ah then – there was Mark, the actor, who was doing some television filming near Towminster but was going back soon to London. Of course this was a wonderful break for Nalini, who'd always wanted to work in London and who'd apparently always thought of going on the stage anyway – 'into the profession', as she now called it. Having only two O levels might be a bit tiresome when it came to getting accepted by a drama school, but Nalini seemed to think that didn't matter. Soon after Mark went back to town, she went there too.

At the time – I suppose I was very naïve, as Nalini herself always said – it puzzled me quite a lot that Nalini had to meet someone like Mark in order to put these ambitions into action. Couldn't she just have *gone* to London like anyone else, I wondered, and got a job and tried enrolling herself at evening classes in acting or something?

It was years before I realised that Nalini is the sort of person who never does anything on her own. That instinct goes so deep in her that I don't think she knows herself that she's like that: she imagines herself to be adventurous and independent. (So did my poor old Mum, who thought Nalini was 'an adventuress' and was shocked when she heard of her doings.) So no wonder Nalini has never liked the idea of my failing to get a man. The prospect that I might spend my life with no one has always filled her with a sort of panic, as if she were afraid not just that I would be lonely (which of course I sometimes am) but that, on my own, I *wouldn't have a life at all*. And so it used to throw me into a panic too, whenever she spoke of it, for years and years – until at last it came to me, not very long ago, that, after all, I wasn't having too bad a life. In fact it had gradually, in an unspectacular way, become rather enjoyable and promising. But I am running ahead . . .

Nalini went to London and wrote me cheerful letters in her big, splashy handwriting about what a fascinating time she was having, meeting all Mark's friends. And, yes, I did envy her, of course. But my own life wasn't too bad: I got my A levels. The grades weren't very good, but I managed to get into a new northern university to study English. In

119

those years I didn't see much of Nalini: she was in London most of the time and I hardly ever went there, even in the holidays, because I had no money – a student grant doesn't go far and of course Mum couldn't afford to help me out as some parents could. Eventually, after I'd left university and done a secretarial course (*much* more 'relevant', I'm afraid, than an Arts degree) I did at last come to the big city and Nalini and I began to meet again.

She wasn't with Mark any longer, and seemed quite cross when I mentioned him. And I don't think she'd ever managed to make her way into what she now called Show Biz. But she seemed to know lots of interesting people in that world and to be having a lively time. We used to meet for lunch sometimes in sandwich bars, and she would tell me about the interesting people she knew, which was nice for her. Of course I could never stay long as I had to get back to the office, which was a bit annoying for Nalini who often had plenty of time in the middle of the day. The evenings were her busy time, she said. I never did quite catch up with all the different jobs she had. At one time she was working in an Arts Club, and at another she was some sort of Girl Friday (well, that's what she said) to a famous author who was working on a novel that was going to blow the lid off the television companies. She was going to accompany him on a working trip to America – or no, wait a minute, wasn't that another man, a journalist? Anyway, for some reason I don't think the trip ever came off.

But she *did* go abroad quite a bit after a while, because I used to get emphatic postcards from her out of the blue from places like Istanbul and Cairo. By that time we had rather lost touch with each other. Our hours, as she said with a cheerful laugh, were so different. I lived right out at the end of the Bakerloo Line – well, it's nice and green out there, and anyway have you seen what rents of flats further into town are like these days? – and the job I now had with this international relief organisation, though very interesting, was tiring: I didn't enjoy late nights, whereas Nalini, as she said, never really got going till after the theatres came out. She'd always made a point of living near the centre: I don't quite know how she managed it. Just lucky, I expect.

I don't know what Nalini did at weekends, but I don't think she'd been home to Towminster for years. Whereas I'd taken to going home as often as I could. Mum's various physical troubles were getting worse, and it was obviously only going to be a matter of time.

But when Mum finally did die – three years ago now: I can still hardly believe it sometimes – I had a letter from Nalini. I suppose that *her* mother, who wasn't a bad sort in her way and had heard Mum was in the hospital, must have written to tell her. Nalini, sounding just like her old warm self (but signing herself Francesca which really threw me for a minute, though I'd recognised her writing at once), wrote to say how sorry she was and what nice memories she had of Mum and so on. Then she went on to say she'd been meaning to write to me anyway – that she was getting married very shortly. She didn't give me any details – Nalini always behaved as if you ought to be up to date with her life even if you couldn't possibly have been – but she ended her letter, 'Salim says that, when we're settled in Lahore, you must come and visit us. Oh do come! I know I'm going to be so happy, but all the same it will be lovely to see old friends.'

Invitations like that must often be issued in the assumption that they will never be taken up. But Nalini wasn't like that: if she didn't want to see you, she wouldn't say she did. And the funny thing was that, just before poor Mum died, I'd been transferred to the section of our organisation which works directly with branches operating in the field. So there was every possibility that, in the future, I might have the opportunity of the trip to the Indian sub-continent and, if so, of course I should be able to pop up to Lahore. I wrote and told 'Francesca' so. That must have been when I had back the first letter signed 'Nalini': it was her new Muslim name.

The opportunity to take her up on her offer did not come right away. I did actually go twice to India for the organisation, once to Delhi and once to Madras, as PA to the area organiser in whose section I'm now working. He wanted me with him because we're used to each other, and can get through a lot of work together, and I must say I did enjoy both trips. But each time I hardly had a day to draw breath (I mean, to go and see the Taj Mahal) let alone pop up to Lahore – quite a complex pop these days in fact, with the Indians and the Pakistanis bristling at each other like tom-cats and no flights except via Karachi.

Finally, just recently, I had some leave owing to me, and the organisation had a meeting in Karachi my boss wanted me to cover. So I was flown out there in the usual way, Club Class, nice (I could get very spoilt like this!), spent my two days in Karachi – and then off to Lahore under my own steam. I did feel quite excited.

One reason, apart from the prospect of seeing Nalini again, was that Lahore was Kipling's town, where *Kim* begins. At college, I'd done my Special Dissertation on Kipling, because my tutor was keen on him, and since then I'd always wanted to see *Kim*'s gun and the Old City of Lahore. People think of Kipling as having written about India, and so it all was of course in his day, but now that northern bit is Pakistan, all self-conscious Islam. I wonder what Kipling would have thought of it? Not much, I suspect.

Nalini came to meet me at the airport. Well, actually she was late – I was standing for some time on the steps, with taxi touts going on at me, not sure myself what to do – and then, suddenly, she was there, waving excitedly from a big car with a driver. I didn't recognise her for a moment, which was stupid of me, but she did look so Pakistani. She's always been dark-haired, you see, and now she'd let it grow long, and she was wearing one of those tunic-and-trousers outfits everyone wears there. I just hadn't expected her to be in Pakistani dress; it gave me a strange feeling I couldn't quite analyse.

It wasn't till I had been there several days that I realised that any European woman living in a traditional city like Lahore more or less has to take to *shalwah-kameez* in self-protection: otherwise you get so stared at you feel uncomfortable wherever you go.

Nalini and the driver and a policeman had some sort of three-cornered argument about whether they ought to have stopped there at all, and meanwhile I got into the car because I couldn't see why we couldn't go on now anyway. Which we eventually did.

The car was air-conditioned and very comfortable, and the driver drove fast along the centre lane, hooting smaller cars, scooter-rickshaws and fairground-painted buses out of the way. I could see already that Nalini's husband must be quite an important man. (As a matter of fact, even though I stayed in his house for a week I never did discover what Salim did. I had thought it was Import-Export, but one time when Nalini was talking about him she made it sound as if he worked for the Government.)

The house, out in a sort of garden suburb, was pretty splendid by anybody's standards, with a sprinkler on the lawn and really lovely flowers and a separate servants' quarter at the back. Inside there was a lot of chromium and glass furniture, which I don't personally care for much (I like something cosier) but you could see it was expensive. There was also an elaborate veneered screen which Nalini said was by the same artist who had done the front hall decor for the Lahore Hilton. (It was very similar too, as I saw when we went to the Hilton for tea.) All in all it was clear right away that Nalini had not made the mistake that I've heard of one or two English girls making – marrying someone from a country like Pakistan, I mean, without realising quite how his family may live back home. There was one girl in our organisation who married a Greek and found herself in a little village house with no running water or electricity, sharing the place with his sisters and a lot of pigs! But there were definitely no pigs here in the Garden Colony. (Well, there wouldn't be, would there, in a country as fiercely Muslim as Pakistan?)

I must say, it did come as rather a surprise to me to find how Muslim and conservative Lahore was. Karachi, the little I saw of it, seemed more like any large city: lots of people around in European clothes, and drinks served at lunchtime in the hotel conference suite. But the whole time

123

in Lahore we never had a drink at all, not even at the party at another house in the Colony where Nalini and Salim took me on Saturday evening: just fruit juice and Seven-Up. I didn't mind for myself, as I've never cared for it much, but I was a bit surprised at Nalini: I mean, she'd been accustomed by her parents to drink from the time she was a child, and when we were young together she used to say 'God, I need a drink' and knock back things like vodka and orange which were much too strong for me. I know Muslims aren't supposed to drink alcohol, but in Karachi as far as I could see lots of them did. I was also surprised, in a different way, when I discovered – but this wasn't till the last day – that Salim did in fact keep bootleg whisky in a drawer to offer to whoever his 'business associates' were; but he never offered any to Nalini.

I thought that perhaps it was because Nalini missed having a drink that she'd taken to eating so many sweet things. She used not to, once she'd left school, because she was always being careful of her figure: she had a tendency to put on weight. Well, now she *had* put on weight. It didn't strike me right away because she still looked quite pretty and because *shalwah-kameez* are becoming to plump ladies, but really that's what she was – plump. In jeans or a tight skirt she would have looked a sight, so it was lucky she didn't wear these things any longer. And it wasn't surprising, because, on both the day after I arrived and the next, we sat in the house most of the time with the manservant bringing us relays of plates with little sugary or spicy snacks on them and glasses of sweet mint tea. It was all very delicious, but nobody needs all that food. I suppose it is the Pakistani way of being polite to the visitor, but in fact Nalini ate much more of it than I did. We sat in her bedroom most of the time with what she called 'the AC' going (the front room only had fans), and she talked and ate, talked and ate, as if she couldn't get enough of either. And I began to feel quite claustrophobic, with the windows shut to keep in all that chilly artificial air, and I wondered if I would ever be let out to see Lahore at all. Salim needed the car both those days, it seemed:

Nalini could only have it, and the driver, when Salim didn't want them.

There was a garden – the Shalimar Gardens – she wanted to take me to see, and on the second day I asked if we couldn't go by bus. And she said, 'Oh heavens, you don't understand, people like us don't take buses here, they're impossible! Salim would be furious if he knew we'd gone on the bus.'

I should have said, 'Well, let's get a taxi, then – I'll pay.' I didn't that day, for some reason. I think it was because I, like Nalini, remembered the old days when she had had money for things like taxis and I didn't. Somehow I didn't like to upset our respective positions.

If I don't say much about Salim it is, as you will probably have gathered, that I didn't take to him much. We don't all have the same tastes in people and just as well; maybe he had – has – all sorts of qualities I don't appreciate. But, though he was polite enough to me, in an oily here-is-our-visitor-from-UK way, I thought he was rude to Nalini. And even ruder to the servants. I know that their ways aren't ours, and so forth, but I still don't think a man as high placed in his own country as Nalini kept saying he was should shout at the gardener.

Fortunately he was very busy with his own affairs, the week I was there, so Nalini and I were left pretty much to our own devices. The third day we did manage to get the car, in the afternoon. Nalini said we should go shopping, and then on to the Shalimar Gardens if there was time.

I said I didn't terribly want to go shopping. (I've got enough clothes, and one or two nice old bits of jewellery Mum left, and I really don't want brightly coloured silks or bangles. I mean, I'd look silly in them, wouldn't I? I'm a Jaeger camel-hair sort of person.) But I said that if Nalini wanted to shop of course I'd go with her, and could it be in the Old City because that's what I particularly wanted to see?

Nalini said the Old City smelt and was full of stall-holders who would try to rob you (neither of which was particularly true, as I later discovered). She said she'd been looking forward to taking me to the new, air-conditioned shopping centre, which was nice and clean and where the shop-keepers knew her. So we went there. We didn't have time for the Shalimar Gardens, that day.

The next day we didn't have the car again, but Nalini suggested we go back to the shopping centre with a friend of hers who lived near and had her own car. This time I'm afraid I was rather firm: I said that I was half way through my visit to Lahore and hadn't even seen Kim's gun yet or the museum where Kipling's father was curator, and that, as far as I was concerned, that was where I was going. Of course Nalini needn't come with me if she had other things to do. (Actually I was hoping she wouldn't. I'd always rather go round a museum on my own.) But Nalini made a great to-do about how I didn't understand and couldn't possibly go anywhere on my own. Then, having made this fuss, of course she had to come with me. We took a taxi.

We had rather an uncomfortable time in the museum because Nalini has never enjoyed things like that and isn't interested in history. But after a while I stopped paying much attention to her. There were some lovely house fronts out of the Old City (which made me want to go and see the place still more) and also the most extraordinary figure of Buddha, not fat like he usually is but emaciated almost to the point of death. He is in fact called the Starving Buddha, I discovered. Every vein and rib and sinew showed and his eyes were like great pits. It's a wonderful piece of work, centuries old; it must have been a very remarkable man who carved it, and I believe he must have had a living – well, barely living – model. Our organisation used photographs of starving children in some of its publicity, but people eventually get annoyed or repelled by that: I couldn't help wondering if we could use the Starving Buddha instead, and whether the Government of Pakistan would let us.

By the time I'd finished thinking about all this, and seen everything else in the museum as well, Nalini was hardly on speaking terms with me.

She cheered up a bit when we finally got to the Shalimar Gardens. The day was cooling off and there were family

126

parties walking about. A group of boys tried to follow us a bit, hopefully saying 'Hallo – how-are-you?' and Nalini said that just showed how absolutely right she'd been not to let me go anywhere on my own. I suspected, however, that if Nalini had not been there talking away and I'd just been walking along in my usual way with my head down the boys would hardly have noticed me.

Nalini said that the Shalimar had once been a summer palace where queens and concubines had lived in purdah – 'What a life, poor dears, never going anywhere.' I didn't say anything.

The next morning Nalini had a class in Japanese flower arrangement. She wanted me to go with her, but I had an excuse ready: I said my tummy was a bit upset. (Well, whose tummy doesn't get a bit upset in these hot countries? But I'm always rattling with pills when I go there, so I manage to keep it – more or less – under control.)

Half an hour after Nalini was safely out of the way, I asked the servant to get me a taxi. That may not sound much like me, but you get used to looking after Number One when you live on your own. And I was getting a bit desperate.

The servant asked where he should tell the taxi to go, and I said, 'the Museum' again as I thought that would sound suitable. But in fact when we got there I asked him to drive on to the Old City; fortunately I'd discovered by then what it's called in Urdu.

It was quite a long way, past markets and the railway station, and at last the driver stopped and waved at a medieval-looking gate in a high wall and made noises, and I understood that he couldn't take the car inside. So there I was.

Well, I won't bore you with it. I know it isn't really very interesting hearing about places where you haven't been, and words like 'old world' and 'picturesque' and 'fascinating' just don't seem to have much life on their own – but, oh, it was all of those things! And the most extraordinary thing for me was the way it was still exactly, but exactly, as it is described in *Kim*, bar a few radios playing and the odd

127

scooter trying to chug its way through the crowds between the ox-carts and hand-carts and the masses of people. I even *recognised* the Street of the Spices Kipling talks about, with the great piles of red, orange, mauve, yellow and white spice shaped into cones. And any one of the boys playing about in the lanes or flying kites on the roofs could have been Kim himself. I know that people say now that Kipling was an Imperialist, but I think he was just a wonderful writer.

Nobody bothered me – oh, except to try to sell me vegetables and live chickens and things as I passed, and of course they were trying to do that to everyone. I was wearng trousers, which is polite in Muslim countries, and a rather voluminous blouse I somehow had felt would be suitable, and a plain scarf on my head, and I hoped I just looked like a relative of the Vicar at the Lahore Anglican church. I think I must have.

I didn't go right into the centre of the City as I was a bit afraid of getting lost. Anyway, I kept seeing interesting things even in the lanes near the gate. I saw a man selling song birds, just like Pappageno in *The Magic Flute*, and another man with a group of children and grown-ups round him watching birds trained to walk up little see-saws and perch on tiny swings. They were very sweet and the man seemed nice. I gave him some money, of course. By the time I got back to the gate and the main road outside it was after half past twelve. I couldn't see a taxi, so I got a rickshaw. The driver seemed rather surprised that I wanted to go all the way to the other side of Lahore, and pretty vague about where the Garden Colony was. I ended up directing him.

Well, you can imagine: (*I* had been able to imagine, but I hadn't let it bother me). When I turned up at Nalini's house she'd been looking out for me – for *hours*, she said, worried *stiff*, she said – and there was a fine old scene.

So ungrateful, she said. And in a rickshaw, of all things. And how did I think she was going to feel, having all their neighbours and Salim's business associates think that she let a guest from England trail around the Old City, of all filthy places, on her own? (So ridiculous; as I said to her, it wasn't as if Salim's business associates or the other rich people from the suburb were lurking behind the stalls in the lanes watching me. Fat chance!)

What puzzled me for a long while was why she was so angry. Not just distressed and worried about me, as she pretended, but really furious. I suppose I shouldn't have been so surprised, all in all, when I came to think about everything, but I was. I imagined for a while that she was mainly hurt because I hadn't wanted to sit and watch her arrange flowers in a Japanese manner. But eventually, after saying various nasty things to me about my general oddness which I won't even repeat, she burst into tears, and I realised that there was more going on than just my being an awkward guest, oh much more.

I stroked her head a bit (her face was buried in the sofa cushions) and did try to say that I knew it must be boring and lonely for her here in Lahore . . . But she shrugged my hand off angrily and I knew then that was the one thing I should not have said. Nalini had never been able to bear that anyone should pity her. It is always her who has to be the one envied, the one admired. That is really necessary to her, somehow. Without that support, she collapses.

At last she said, snuffling into her hanky:

'And I haven't had a baby, you see . . .'

Stupidly, that aspect of the situation hadn't even occurred to me. Nalini had never seemed to care much for children in the old days. But of course that was beside the point if Salim wanted them – or wanted to prove his wife could have them. I could see at once how awful it must be for Nalini if no baby was appearing.

With her face half in the cushion, she said – no, she cried, it really was a cry:

'He says that if I don't get pregnant soon he'll divorce me.'

I sat and stroked her head a bit more. I guessed I should really have embarked on a helpful female conversation with her about gynaecology and perhaps going to a Western-trained specialist in Karachi, but that sort of thing has never been much in my line. And anyway, the more I considered

129

it, the more I thought it would be better if Salim and she did *not* have a child together.

At last I said:

'Well, if it comes to that point – why don't you leave *him* before he can do that to you? Why don't you go back to England?'

She said, sort of shuddering:

'Oh, I can't do that. You don't understand, a Muslim wife can't ever do that –'

'But you're *not* a Muslim wife,' I heard myself say rather angrily. I suppose I did suddenly feel quite angry with Nalini, as well as desperately sorry for her. I could see she was afraid all over, in just that kind of mindless, paralysing way that I used once to be, long ago, when she seemed to know more than I did. I said:

'You're not a Muslim and this isn't your country. All this silly pretence about being Pakistani when you've nothing to do here, absolutely nothing . . . You're an independent English woman who's had jobs and led a proper life – well, a life worth living, anyway. Go back to that, for goodness sake, while there's still time!' I added on a sudden afterthought:

'If you haven't the money for the fare, I'll gladly lend it to you.'

She didn't accept, not right away. But she calmed down after that and blew her nose and said what a good friend I'd always been to her. And we ended up having a long, cosy talk about when we were kids together in Towminster, although in all the years between she'd never seemed to want to recall that much: she's even made out she can't remember it.

She hardly mentioned Salim again, either then or for the rest of my stay. And I hardly saw him again either, except when there were other people there.

Now I'm back in England I haven't heard from her yet, but I do seriously expect to. Nalini has never been one just to sit and rot – as she herself once used to put it.

I'm worried about her. I think in fact she may have quite a difficult time getting free from Salim, who won't like to lose face. But I'm not *that* worried. Nalini will pop up again in the end, with another name, not too badly damaged. Nalini will survive, of that I am sure. She is a survivor. That is her role in life, and her secret.

As a matter of fact I rather suspect I am a survivor too. Perhaps that is the reason we've remained friends all these years, when it seems so unlikely that we should be? But she knew from the beginning that she was a survivor; it has taken me years and years to learn it, and even then I am one in a very different way from her. Somehow I have to do everything for myself. Perhaps that is the real difference between us.

In a Past Life

Julia was brought up in Maidstone, England, in the 1960s, but she always knew – from early in her teens, that she must be meant for a different sort of life.

Julia was quite pretty, in a plump way, and once she stopped eating sweets both her figure and her complexion improved. She had long, light-brown hair, which she wore loose at school though her mother and the older teachers wanted her to plait it. Later, when her mother suggested she might cut it short and perm just the ends, Julia continued to take no notice and used to plait it, wet, into tight little braids that dried in long crinkles like one of those pictures by that painter – Julia could never remember his name. It was very easy to take no notice of her mother, Julia thought, since she didn't know anything. Why, poor Mummy wondered why Julia didn't join the Young Conservatives, of all things, and had paid for Julia to have extra tennis coaching at school because she thought it would be 'a social asset, darling', not realising that the only reason Julia wanted it was that she fancied the tennis coach. Julia supposed that poor old Mummy, being a widow, had forgotten ages ago about fancying people, and now of course it was too late for that – or for anything else. Julia was conscious that life was full of exciting possibilities, and *she* wasn't going to get bogged down in a place like Maidstone. That was why, although fancying – first the tennis coach and then a long series of other people – occupied most of Julia's waking thoughts for a number of years, she wasn't going to make the mistake of marrying for ages yet. Not her! She was destined for other things.

Julia got a place at a university in the Midlands, where she began on European Literature, because that was what was suggested to her, and then changed to Social Anthropology. She left at the end of her second year, having

133

failed an exam twice, because anyway (as she said) it was really a bit pointless, wasn't it? After all, it was *life* she was interested in, not immature academic studies. A year before she would have said 'stuffy old books', but her time at College had sharpened her vocabulary. Most of the bourgeois shibboleths were immature (Julia now knew) compared with the real business of living. And she was all set for that to begin.

But it didn't – not really. Of course it was quite *fun* in London, where she now crashed in someone else's pad in Chalk Farm and even, after a while, managed to get a job selling programmes at the Roundhouse. It was really nice feeling you were at the centre of things, sort of, particularly when she had this chap Ron, who worked on a stall in the Camden Lock market: Julia felt then that she had arrived at last. But where had she arrived? She wasn't quite sure; and sometimes, sweeping down the Chalk Farm Road in her long, tie and dyed cotton skirt, feeling her kinked hair lying warm and lovely between her shoulder blades, Julia felt, in spite of everything, uncertain and still obscurely waiting for everything to begin.

Julia's mother worried, on the rare occasions Julia went home for the weekend: she was afraid her daughter might be on drugs; one read such awful things in the papers . . . This made Julia laugh. Of course she knew people who smoked pot more or less all the time but, although she pretended to go along with the whole scene just so as not to feel left out, secretly Julia was bored by it. When people were high they might seem happy and relaxed and friendly, but they weren't really paying attention to you at all. Julia preferred people to pay attention to her.

But it was through some of Ron's smoking friends that she first heard about India. Of course that wasn't strictly true: she'd heard of it before at school (the Black Hole of Calcutta, which had also been the name of one of the school lavatories) and there were those Oxfam posters, and also she'd been wearing Indian jewellery for simply *ages*: the stall next to Ron's sold it, and she had a whole lot of silver bangles and some earrings and a toe-ring. But somehow

134

none of this had made India real to her: she hadn't been aware, as it were, of the place waiting for her, her own peculiar personal destiny, till the plan emerged about Dave's van.

Ron's mate Dave had this Dormobile that he was planning to drive all the way to Katmandu, taking in Europe, the Middle East, Afghanistan and India on the way. You could still do that, in 1972. It sounded fun, and Julia managed, as she said, to get a little bread together (actually from her mother, as a twenty-first birthday present) and was all set to go. Ron wouldn't come: he said he couldn't let the stall go now, or something stuffy and irrelevant, and that anyway it was bound to work out more expensive than Dave said, and *anyway* he didn't really dig all that stuff about the Bhagvad Gita. And he went out of Julia's life in a huff.

But Julia dug it, all of it – the Bhagavad Gita, the Upanishads (which sounded so profound quoted in small bits in Dave's resonant northern voice) *and* all those temple carvings which, as Dave said, showed how wonderfully untainted by Western capitalist hang-ups about sex the Indians were. Actually, if the truth were told, Dave's own sexual performance didn't seem to have quite that easy, untrammelled quality that he professed to admire in Shiva and Parvati, and he could also be a bit jealous in a boring, humpy, sour-faced way. But quite a lot of them were going in the van, six or seven, so Julia guessed that there wouldn't be all that much opportunity for Dave to practise on her. She was rather relieved at this. Although she would never have admitted it, even to herself, Julia found sexual intercourse was not all that people made out it was. She preferred talking about it.

They set off at last and, as Ron had predicted, the journey took far longer than Dave had said it would, and far more things went wrong. After the van had broken down for the fourth time – in Turkey, that was – two people left the party to hitchhike back to Athens, and they had to leave another in the hospital at Tabriz with some sort of rotten stomach bug. (But that was his own fault, thought Julia: he should

135

have stuck to yogurt and rice and vegetables like she did – meat was poison, everyone knew *that*.) Then, going over the Khyber Pass, she and Dave, who'd been bickering for weeks, had a final ghastly row about *money*, of all silly, unimportant things – who owed who what. Julia was a bit ashamed of that afterwards; it did seem rather a let-down to be arguing about that, and the worst of it was she had been so annoyed by Dave's insistence that they all ought to go shares on repairs to the van that she hadn't really seen the Khyber Pass at all, which was a pity when it was supposed to be one of the world's wonders, wasn't it?

The result of all this quarrelling and being cooped up for weeks in that beastly van, with everyone stinking and smoking pot and making feebler and feebler jokes, was that Julia couldn't *wait* to get away from them all. Once in Lahore, in the Y, she left them having showers, took her own bundle and sleeping bag and exactly half her and Dave's joint money (that'd teach him to be so petit bourgeois about it!) and walked out on her own. She went to the station and caught the train to Amritsar across the frontier and thence to Bombay, where she happened to have an introduction to some friends of friends of her mother's.

Julia liked Bombay. She had been too intent on leaving the others in Lahore to notice the place much, and the smaller towns through which they had passed in the north had intimidated her: so had the endless, dusty landscapes seen from the windows of the train. In spite of vegetarianism and the simple life, Julia did not actually like the country much: whether it was Kent or the Rajasthan desert it all seemed a bit dull and also difficult to live in. Life in cities was far easier and more fun. When Julia arrived in Bombay she at once felt at home; it was almost like *recognising* the place (as she later told people she met there). Since Bombay was built largely by the British, after the style of London and Manchester, her feeling was not unusual, but this explanation did not occur to Julia. Instead, she concluded she might have lived in Bombay before, in a past life, for by that time she had got really interested in reincarnation.

136

Hindus believed in it, so she understood, and, really, it made a lot of sense, didn't it? The beggar on the corner with a twisted leg, or the family with four children living on the pavement opposite didn't worry about their present predicament because they knew that this world was just a phase and that the next life would make up for this one. That, thought Julia, was why they were all so marvellously calm and seemed to sleep such a lot. Among the crowds on the pavements, in between the hooting traffic and the jumble of bullock-carts and hand-carts, she herself moved as in a happy dream – or in a film.

She quickly got to know a lot of people in Bombay. A girl she met at the Salvation Army hostel on her first night took her to a PR reception at the Taj Hotel – a lot of the foreigners at the Sally used the Taj as a coffee shop and general meeting place – and there she met Premchand, who was something to do with the Raj Kamal Film Studios, and he asked her to a party two nights later, so then she was off. It was lovely being so popular. She *felt* more interesting in Bombay than she had in London, and here people seemed to have plenty of time to listen to her. Having a cheerful nature, she loved talking to people about how happy she was in Bombay, and extolling even those aspects of the city of which the permanent inhabitants seemed less than proud. She began explaining, at the buffet suppers to which she was presently invited, that it was the *people* of Bombay she loved – just the ordinary, simple people who were so beautiful in their ordinary cotton saris and dhotis and had so much natural taste. Sometimes, if she were feeling a little bit aggressive, she would add 'so much more beautiful than the rich'. It was fun to talk like that, in someone's grand living room.

Once she made the mistake of saying this in front of another Englishman, at a party in a big, air-conditioned apartment on Malabar Hill. He was rather a dreary man (she had already decided) who worked for some international firm, and he reminded her uncomfortably of a doctor they had once had in Maidstone who had told her mother that she – Julia – ought to eat fewer sweets and more green salads. Now he said, looking at her, in the same cold-eyed British way:

'The reason the people in the streets here wear bright orange and emerald green and so forth is to do with caste – nothing to do with innate taste. Higher caste Hindus don't wear these colours. Everything is laid down in Indian life – individual autonomy hardly exists here. If you haven't understood that, you will never understand anything about India.'

That made Julia quite cross, because she had got used, here in Bombay, to being someone who really felt for the poor and empathised with them which was something that she had noticed Premchand and his friends did not do. Premchand used to talk – he talked a lot – about the Poverty Problem and the Population Problem, but really, she suspected, he did not like the poor and rather wished they weren't there. So she always made a point of saying how much she loved them and how at home she felt when she was wandering for hours in the bazaars, and most of the people she met seemed to think well of her for that – nice, generous, easy-going people like Premchand, not cold-eyed Englishmen. At the time, she couldn't think of an answer to the Englishman, and just moved crossly off to the buffet. (The food at these parties was simply marvellous: Julia always ate *tons*, and then hardly needed to eat at all at other times – just a cup of tea, or a handful of roast peanuts off a stall like any ordinary person, which of course was a great saving.)

But afterwards she thought she ought to have said scathingly to him: oh, I suppose *you* think that the people living freely in the streets doing their own thing ought to be swept up by some busybodying Council and stuck into tower-blocks with hot and cold running water and petty restrictions about dogs and lodgers and ball-games . . . And then he would have said, trying to answer . . . And then she would have said . . .

She particularly liked the way some of the families camping on the pavements kept dogs: it seemed so nice and domestic. She mentioned this once to Premchand and his

138

friend Vikram, and they both laughed in the way they did when they were a bit disconcerted. They were easy to disconcert, and thought Julia tremendously original. After a moment, Premchand said:

'Hah! They do it to keep the rats away from their children . . . Haven't you seen the sewer rats here, Julia?' And Vikram said, screwing up his mouth in an Oriental, faintly womanish way he had:

'Dogs aren't very clean to us, you see, isn't it? My family, for instance, wouldn't keep a dog . . . It is not our custom.'

Julia had always liked dogs, ever since she hadn't been allowed to have one when she was a child, so of course what Vikram said just made her feel all the more that the simple people of Bombay were the ones with the right ideas on how to live. Meanwhile, one way and another, she had been in Bombay over three weeks before she actually got round to visiting these friends of friends of her mother's. They lived in a suburb called Bandra, and Julia's Bombay social antennae were now sufficiently developed for her to know that this was not smart, or anyway not smart like Malabar Hill or Marine Drive or the Taj Hotel, although of course it was still worlds away from the industrial blocks and shanty towns on the dock side of the city. All the same, it was a long, hot ride out there on a particularly full bus, and then Julia (who had got rather used to Premchand's car) took ages to find the right building. Everyone she asked said something different, and waggled their heads in that maddening way, so that she got crosser and crosser and would have felt like killing them (except of course that, she reminded herself, she loved them really) and when she finally got to the right place she found it wasn't a party and that no one had been invited except herself.

Mr and Mrs Pedder were very nice, decent people, and Julia could see that they would have got on frightfully well with her mother, but she began to wish almost at once that she had not come. They were Mission School teachers, retired early because of Indianisation, but although they had elected to stay on in Bombay and work for some voluntary organisation Julia didn't think it was because they actually liked the place. From the way they talked about it – the sickness, the poverty, the unending needs – it was almost as if they hated it, and their flat was like a little oasis of England: it might have been in Maidstone. For supper – but the Pedders called it Tea, and had obviously been waiting with some impatience for Julia's delayed arrival – they had corned beef and salad, and then bottled pears and custard. They didn't keep a servant, Mrs Pedder explained, because they didn't really think it right to keep servants, and anyway of course Indian ways weren't quite their own – 'though we did have a dear old bearer at the Mission, didn't we, Father?'

In England, Julia would as a matter of course spoken scathingly of anyone who said that keeping servants was OK – after all, it was simply exploitation, wasn't it – but here in India it seemed such a normal and natural thing to have people to wait on you that she couldn't help feeling just a *little* patronising towards the servantless Pedders and wondering if it was actually lack of money that stopped them from employing anyone – or British meanness. (Premchand and Vikran said that it was a duty to employ people if you could afford to, and no one could accuse them of being mean, at any rate towards Julia.)

Julia ate the corned beef, as some whisper from her childhood warned her that it would be rude and pointless to make an issue about vegetarianism here, in this tiny flat with its reproductions of Constable and Turner, but she did not enjoy her supper. It was made worse, she told herself, by the fact that, for the last day or two, she had had some sort of silly stomach bug. She knew that her mother would have thought tonight's meal just the thing to set her right again, but Julia didn't agree. 'Tomorrow,' she thought, consoling herself and thinking how well she was behaving, 'I'll have a good, hot onion *utapam* and a bowl of curd. I'll feel better then. And perhaps I *should* drink only boiled water or soda for a day or two, like Premchand says . . . I bet it's boiled here, anyway . . .'

But in spite of her polite behaviour the Pedders were, she gradually realised, rather shocked by her. They had

140

evidently keyed themselves up (poor old things – their lives must be as dull as their food) to entertain a lonely English girl, a stranger to Bombay, and were taken aback by her industriously sustained chatter about friends and parties, the Taj and Gaylords, the film studios and the stars. Julia began to wish, as the meal was ending with a cup of weak nescafé, that she hadn't tried quite so hard to entertain *them*, but it was too late now to stop and pretend to be somebody different, and anyway why should she? Stifling a slight nausea – that revolting custard! Just like school – she talked on.

The Pedders were also more than a little shocked, it seemed, by her bare feet. Julia realised now she should have put on sandals to come here, but she simply had not thought to do so. She hardly ever wore them these days: bare feet had become her hallmark, one of the original details that made people at the parties and studios notice her. It showed, she felt, her essential identification with the poor.

But here was silly old Mrs Pedder telling her she shouldn't, just as if she was her *mother* or something and thought she had a right to tell her what not to do –

'. . . It really isn't safe, dear. You can pick up some quite nasty things from the dirty pavements, you know.'

'But masses of people never wear anything on their feet,' said Julia in her most unhelpful voice.

'Well, poor people, no, they don't. The very poor, that is, coolies and so forth. But anyone who can afford a pair of sandals wears them, they'd be ashamed not to, and of course they're quite right . . . Cleanliness and decency *do* matter – that is, if you're lucky enough to be able to manage them with so much squalor all round . . . We've seen parents pay out money they can ill afford, just to make sure a child doesn't go barefoot, haven't we, George . . .?' Mrs Pedder's voice trailed off uncertainly, suppressing irritation.

George Pedder sucked at his pipe in silence. He wanted to tell this girl (but of course he wouldn't) that people like her – going round with no shoes on, with dirty feet and long, crumpled cotton garments and raggedy bits and bobs

141

like a gipsy – made a mockery both of genuine destitution and of the valiant struggles of Indian clerks and artisans to attain something a bit better for themselves and their families. George Pedder loved the Indians, though not their country, and had devoted his life to helping them, and it made him wordlessly angry to see this new generation of Westerners coming out here with their scruffy degenerate ways, apeing poverty while not knowing the first thing about it. Not knowing a thing about anything, apparently. People like this little girl didn't seem to know they were born . . . What rubbish was she talking now?

'. . . And my friend Premchand says that I've taken to going barefoot so naturally that I must have done it in a past life. Of course I tell him I was an Indian in a past life – just an ordinary peasant, no one grand. No, really! I mean, it started as a joke, but I do actually *feel* now that it is true. I mean, reincarnation must be true, that's obvious . . .'

'But my dear. . . ! That isn't Christian belief. On the contrary. My dear child, even if you aren't a practising Christian (and I know a lot of you young people aren't) I do think you should be *very* wary of getting mixed up with these unchristian beliefs . . . You never know *quite* what you're getting into, you see.'

Eventually Julia managed to leave. She felt unaccountably exhausted, and also rather fed up. Why should they think they can patronise me? she thought crossly. Silly old things, what do they know: they're just the sort who are afraid of everything, and don't like it when other people aren't . . . Contemplating her own achievement in being afraid of nothing these days, she felt a little better. But she mistook the bus number and got on the wrong one, which carried her to a part of Bombay she did not know. She got off, and walked quickly and directionlessly through the badly lighted streets, which were nearly empty of traffic but almost as full of people as they were in the day. The street families were settling down in rows on their pitches, some cooking their evening meal on tiny charcoal braziers, others already wrapping themselves and their children in cloths ready for the night on the pavement. Julia was not afraid of

142

them, even the dirtiest and most disreputable-looking. It seemed right and companionable for them to be there.

At last, after walking a long way, she caught another bus which took her as far as the Victoria Terminus, and then walked the rest of the way to the Sally. She crept on to her bed there without waking the other girls in the room and fell asleep at once.

Two hours later, she was suddenly awake again. After a few minutes of increasing uneasiness – for the first time since she had come to Bombay she did feel fear, a kind of formless dread – she made a dash for the bathroom down the hall and was violently sick.

'That bloody corned beef,' she said to herself, lying faint and sweating on the tiled floor. But even as she said it, she knew her illness could not possibly be just that. After a few minutes another bout of nausea seized her, and as she retched over the lavatory pan her bowels also contracted helplessly. Shivering, dirty, gasping for breath and half crying, she went on lying there, and for the very first time in her life the fear of dying entered her mind.

She was alone, and in pain and desperate and no one, it seemed, had heard her. Another disgusting, terrifying bout swept over her. She rather thought she was bringing up blood now, but was not sure under the sickly neon light. After a while, she fainted.

A long time later, so it seemed, she began to wake. Consciousness returned by degrees, making certain things real and present while much was still blotted out.

It was dark now, but she was still lying on a hard surface. She could feel it under her head, and her hip . . . But was 'still' the word? Should it not be 'again'? How much time had passed? It seemed like a lifetime.

She was conscious, too, by degrees, of dirt and stuffiness. But this place was somehow cramped, not like the other had been. And this time she was not alone.

She stretched out a hand in the stuffy, peopled dark – which was not entirely dark, nor yet silent, for there were continual murmurs and movements. Somewhere near a

143

baby was crying, and somewhere too a person was moaning. Was either of them herself? She was not sure.

Her hand touched crumpled cloth, another body that heaved and shifted away. Her fingers trailed across the bumpy hardness beneath her. A rat scuttled, somewhere very near.

In her nostrils was a scent of dust – dust and burnt charcoal and spice, overlaid by diesel fumes and urine. The scent of the streets, of Bombay, of India, of her life from now on. In one searing flash, before the shutter of time came down, closing the black pit between one knowledge and another, one life and the next, she knew both where she was and where she was not, what she had been and what she must henceforth be.

Never again the cool skies, never again beds and sheets, never again the green grass and flowers, the abundant, flowing waters. Never again England. Never again the Taj Hotel or the Raj Kamal Studios or an air-conditioned apartment on Malabar Hill, never again sumptuous meals or boiled, iced water, or shoes, or servants to bring you things or hospitals with nurses in white, or people to help and look after you and give you money on which to live your own life – Never again, Julia.

From now on there would be only the heat and dust, the dirt and the sounds and the smells, the rats and the passing cars, the streets in the aching dawn, in the heat of midday, in the fetid dark, when the monsoons came . . . And beneath her body the pavement, for ever and ever, till the other end of time.

The shutter descended.

Faith

'Oh why', asked Georgina, 'could you not have let them live? *Why?*' she repeated, almost angrily.

The small lead Madonna looked sulky. Perhaps she was tired of holding her plump infant aloft to the unresponsive woods; Or maybe she was simply tired of the procession of whining human beings demanding favours of her over the years. But probably, Georgina decided, there were fewer of those than there had once been. Life moved faster today: it was 1919. Cars were multiplying on the roads even in this remote part of the country, and the farm-hands and their lumpy girls had other ideas than praying for their hearts' desire to a Lady of lead and stone. It was, as everyone said, the War that had done it. Evidently the War had had all sorts of sinister magic powers, besides the central one of removing from life Georgina's only son Raymond.

The War had, in a sense, removed her husband too, but Georgina did not regard that bereavement as in the same class as the loss of Raymond. Charles had been fifty-five in 1915 when he had dropped dead from a heart attack which kind friends hastened to attribute to 'wartime overwork' but which Georgina knew quite well was due, rather, to obesity and uncertain temper. She had mourned him sincerely – after all, a husband is a husband, and she would miss him for all sorts of reasons – and when, in the early summer of 1918, in one of the last great slaughters of the War, Raymond had been removed too, she had agreed readily with those friends, who said, 'At least poor Charles was spared this sad day . . .' But, since 1915, she had thought very little of Charles, whereas Raymond, killed a year ago today, had been, literally, always in her thoughts.

'Why?', she repeated censoriously to the Madonna. Her tone was not so much agonised as accusing. It was almost as if she were telling the Lady, 'You have made things very

145

difficult for yourself by this oversight: how will you sort the matter out?' It was inconceivable that gifted, handsome Raymond, not to mention his almost equally gifted school-friend Laurence, should have died meaninglessly, by mere vulgar ill-fortune, as a million and a half other British soldiers had died, in mud and obscurity. (Georgina counted only the British dead.) No, Raymond and Laurence's deaths, however terrible, must be part of some complex, yet-to-be-revealed pattern: to think otherwise would be insupportable.

It was the Roman Catholicism in which Georgina had been reared that made her so certain on this point. Both Charles and she had come from Old Catholic families, the kind that had subsisted in England in quiet comfort for generations, debarred by their faith from public office but content in a deep awareness of their own spiritual invincibility. They cultivated their lands, sent their sons to universites abroad, occasionally married their daughters into foreign, impeccably Catholic families. Even though times had changed the traditions still subsisted, as if the old families rejected the toleration now extended to them. Raymond himself would probably have been sent to Heidelberg had the War not supervened, and Georgina had even had her eye on a pretty second cousin for him in the French branch of the family. Waste, tragic waste . . . No, certainly, the Lady, or rather the ultimate celestial arbiter whom she represented, must have some further revelation in store. Of that, Georgina was obscurely but resolutely certain.

However the Faith which gave her this certitude also posed a problem. Since that terrible day a year ago when the telegram had come, her dominant thought, which was with her every morning when she woke and last thing at night after she had said her prayers, was that death was after all surmountable. It was only a veil between this world and the next, and such a veil – surely – Raymond of all people would have the will and ingenuity to penetrate. He was taking his time, certainly; but he would assuredly reach her – make some sign to her of his continuing existence. He *must*.

146

However, (as Georgina, a cradle Catholic, well knew), such signs were looked on askance by the Church. One was assured the veil was only a veil, told there was absolutely no doubt about the Life Everlasting and even the Resurrection of the Body – and yet, so to speak, telegrams, letters and signs of affection between the other side of the veil and this were apparently forbidden. It seemed very illogical. Raymond had always written such good letters too, from school, from France, full of descriptions of his daily life and solicitude for hers. For two years of war he had written frequently, even when at the Front: in death he would never, she knew, have willingly left her like this without a sign . . . So why should he now be prevented from communicating with her, his mother? It was enough to make one (almost) lose faith in that perfect Love all human love transcending . . . Or could the Church possibly have got it wrong?

She had made enquiries, and it appeared that Protestants, those semi-atheists of whom she knew little, were allowed much more liberty in communicating with the dead, even to attending seances for the purpose . . . She was tempted to wonder if, after all, another form of Christianity might have something to be said for it. Now that Charles was dead, and she had no one to please but herself . . . Except her brother Simon, and he, living in eccentric bachelorhood in Norfolk, hardly counted. Not that she would *advertise* any change, of course . . .

However she had hopes of today. The Church paid considerable attention to anniversaries, let it pay attention to this one. She had made a declaration of anger to the statuette: let Them make her some answer. She returned to her large, comfortable, silent house in militant mood, thinking at the same time that she really must speak to the gardener, about the untidiness of the lower herbaceous border.

Entering the little morning-room where she commonly sat when on her own – and it was seldom that she was not on her own these days – her attention was suddenly arrested. The vase of early marigolds that had been on the round table earlier that day had been moved to her bureau.

147

Yet the room had already been done by the maids that morning before she had been in it. She had written letters at the bureau before going to walk in the woods.

Outwardly, and even to herself, she remained calm. But her heart began to beat much faster than usual, and thus she knew that something of tremendous import had occurred.

Marigolds had been Raymond's favourite flower. Or rather, he had always expressed himself amused and touched by their 'wonderful vulgarity'. Wonderful indeed. And surely these in the vase were more glowing than when she had left them, as if vibrant with a secret life?

Trembling with inner excitement, Georgina sat quietly down in her fireside chair, hands folded in her lap, to await a further sign.

Shortly before it was time for luncheon the bell at the front of the house rang. Georgina jumped violently, as if the sound had been much louder than it really was, but naturally remained seated.

The maid appeared: 'A gentleman, M'm.' Georgina looked automatically for a silver tray and a card, but there was none.

'Did he give his name?'

'No, M'm. But he asked for you. Said he had a message for you.'

'Show him in.'

Young. Tall. Not bad-looking but moved awkwardly. Dressed like a gentleman. Needed a haircut. Could he really be the bearer of the Sign for which she was waiting? Stifling a rising disappointment – Georgina had never been accustomed to show her feelings before strangers, or even before intimates, for that matter – she murmured sympathetically. '*Do* sit down,' and arranged herself in an attitude of listening expectancy.

The young man sat, with an awkward alacrity. In a voice that seemed educated but slightly strangulated, as if he had some speech impediment, he said:

'I didn't give your maid my name. Servants tend to get it wrong, I find . . . But perhaps you recognise me?'

She hesitated. She felt his yearning that she should say

148

yes, and indeed there *was* something about him . . . But no. She really could not honestly say she knew who he was.

'I'm sorry,' she said.

'Ah, I thought you might not. I know I've changed a good deal. I've been through a lot this year . . . It's Laurence. Laurence de la Foy – Raymond's friend . . . Surely you recognise me *now*, Mrs Laidlow?'

As he went on to explain, she studied him carefully. Dark hair and eyes, fresh complexion, bony face . . . Yes it *could* be Laurence. If he had lost a certain amount of boyish flesh and also grown several inches this last year . . . And, come to think of it, it must be a good three years since she had seen Laurence, at that last Prize Day at Downside. A man, let alone a boy barely out of his teens, could change a good deal in three years. And, thinking further, she had probably never met him more than four times altogether. She had always felt she knew him well, because Raymond used to talk about him a lot, and then after the boys had been killed she had corresponded with his poor mother and they had exchanged photos and memories . . . But she had only ever met him to talk to briefly; he had never stayed here, at Laidlow Court. There had been talk of him doing so, she rather thought, but Raymond had never really wanted school friends about in his precious holiday time. He and she had been so close, and that was their time together . . .

Still uncertain, but increasingly convinced it must be as the young man said – for why should he lie? – she studied this Laurence returned from the dead. But no, not apparently dead after all – he was explaining everything to her:

'. . . And so, after we escaped from the prison camp, I found my way back to France. To Paris, actually. Last November. The Armistice had just been signed and everything was in such a muddle it wasn't hard to slip through . . . I found myself a job. Washing up in a restaurant. Yes, hard work. But I'm not afraid of that. At least it's kept me from starving.'

'But I don't understand', she said, not for the first time.

'Why haven't you made yourself known to the authorities – to the War Office – to your family? They still believe you are dead!'

'I thought I had explained all that,' he said patiently. (He was a patient young man, she could see that.) 'How can I make myself known just like that? I told you about our miraculous escape, but Raymond and I are technically deserters, as I said. And the Defence of the Realm Act has not yet been repealed. If we were both to come out of hiding now we could still be – shot. In cold blood. At dawn, you know.'

Her hand went to her face in horror. He half smiled, as if he had known it would – or as if he had faced all this within himself and come to terms with it.

'You say my Raymond *is* still alive?' she asked, when she had recovered her composure.

'He certainly was when I last saw him, on the road to Bruges. As I said, we went our separate ways. It seemed – safer.'

'And – he's likely to have survived since?'

'Well, I have survived, haven't I? said Laurence gently. It quieted her beating heart when he spoke like that, smiled like that. She could see now why Raymond had thought so much of him.

'You must remember, though,' he added still more gently, 'that, as I said, he has been wounded. Shell-shocked, and wounded in the face. I tell you this so that if – when – you see him again you find him changed, you will not be too upset. But he is still your son.'

She said slowly, mainly to herself: 'This explains everything.' She really meant: this explains why Raymond did not try to reach me through the veil of death. He was not dead at all, so how could he?

That he might, even in hiding, have tried to reach her through the normal postal services, was a commonplace thought she did not care to explore. Georgina was not a commonplace person.

The young man seemed to relax. He smiled at her lovingly, then asked, 'Do you mind awfully if I smoke? My nerves, you know . . . since we were both buried in that shell-hole . . .'

She said ceremonially: 'I have to thank you for saving my son's life.'

He replied at once: 'Oh, he would have done the same for me.'

Yes, that was the authentic tone of their schoolboy closeness! She recognised it from Raymond's own letters. Yet something still worried her. She said:

'But what I don't quite understand – Oh, do excuse me; there are some here in this box.' For Laurence, having mentioned cigarettes, was now patting each of his pockets in turn as if he had forgotten his own.

'Turkish this side,' she said, 'Virginian the other.'

He took one, lit it. (It struck a very faintly wrong note that he did not offer the box to her, but no doubt, she told herself, he assumed she did not smoke.) Then, inhaling like a man who has wanted a cigarette for some time, he said:

'I expect you're going to ask me why I've come first to you rather than to my own mother?'

It was not anything as specific as that which was worrying Georgina, but now he mentioned it – 'Yes, why have you?' she asked.

'Well, as I told you, I'm still technically a deserter. In hiding. So is Raymond. That, I'm sure, is why he has stayed in France. And my own home is exactly where the military authorities might be looking for me. So I decided to come first to you instead . . .'

'But the authorities believe you to be dead,' said Georgina promptly. 'Your poor mother had a telegram from the War Office, as I did. It said *Missing, Presumed Dead.*'

'Yes, but my mother has never believed that,' he said equally promptly. 'I expect you knew that.'

'Well . . . It was very hard to believe. Of course one goes on hoping against hope. Rightly, as it turns out!' She smiled at him, wanting to cry, to take his hands in hers, wanting to embrace him as if he had been Raymond himself. Yet something in his gentle, assured yet oddly remote manner

151

held her back. Did not people say indeed that the men who survived the full horror of the War and returned from it were mysteriously changed, set apart in some way from their former loved ones, as if returned from the land of death itself. Would Raymond be like this too? *And shell-shocked . . . And wounded in the face . . .* If so, she must accept it.

'I expect you saw this,' Laurence said.

She looked down, and found he was holding out to her a newspaper cutting. It was in French, and it said that Mrs Noreen de la Foy would welcome any information on her son, 2nd Lt. Laurence de la Foy, 14th Rifles, or on his friend Lt. Raymond Laidlow, 14th Rifles, both believed to be still alive somewhere in France or Belgium. It gave home addresses for both boys.

'No,' she said slowly, 'I didn't know about this.'

How typical of poor Norrie, was her first, unworthy thought. A newspaper advertisement – really! Then, immediately afterwards, came a gush of humility and gratitude that Norrie had had the hardihood and – yes – the faith, to use such a means to an end. For if the boys were really found alive . . .

Of course they were! Here, already, was Laurence. And he was promising to track down Raymond for her. He knew just where, in Belgium, to look, he said. He would have done so already had he not been absolutely broke. Really, only just about able to keep body and soul together at all by this wretched washing-up job – and he had let that go and used his last franc coming to England to see her. 'I hitched lifts in farmers' carts the last part of the journey from Dover,' he confessed. 'That's why I look a bit scruffy.'

This boyish frankness of his disarmed her – if, indeed, she had any armament left. She gave him all the money she had: four pounds, ten shillings from her handbag, and another twenty pounds that she always kept in reserve in her desk drawer.

'Now I feel more than ever honour-bound to find poor Raymond for you,' he said. 'In fact, I start now.'

152

'But are you sure,' she said, still obscurely troubled in some area of her being that she could not identify, 'that you won't at least contact your mother while you are in England. After all, she still fears you may be dead! Won't you at least let me telephone her from here to give her the wonderful news? You could speak to her –'

'Please, please don't, I beg you,' he said earnestly, almost urgently. 'I have told you how dangerous my position is. Would you want my poor mother to find me again only to see me arrested and – shot? No, no, let me escape abroad again. I tell you, I shan't rest now till I have found Raymond for you, and have at last got a message from him to you. And, for my own safety – and Raymond's too, of course – I must ask you not to mention this visit to anyone. No one at all. Not even yet to my mother. Poor mother. She might – do something rash. You promise, Mrs Laidlow?'

She promised.

The lunch-gong sounded and she asked him if he would not stay to eat, but he refused. She offered a drink – a cup of tea at least? – instead, but he would not stay. Clearly he was very anxious and felt the need to be gone.

'I'll show you out myself,' she said.

As her hand was on the door of the morning-room, he said hurriedly:

'I hate to mention the subject again, Mrs Laidlow, but if it *does* take me some time to find Raymond I might need . . .'

'Of course,' she said, at once understanding and embarrassed for him. 'If – that is, do you have a bank account? Oh no, how stupid of me, of course you can't have at the moment.'

'An international postal order to Poste Restante at the main post office in Ostend would find me,' he said.

Again she promised.

After he had gone she went into the dining-room, where her cold luncheon was arranged for her on a lace cloth, but she did not eat. She sat with her hands in her lap apparently looking out on to the sunlit lawns. But an observer, had there been anyone to observe, would have said that she was looking, rather, into some region within herself.

153

It is possible that, for the first time in a year, she saw the future. If so, it was a shadowed and strange one, bearing little relation to the sunlit futures she had been accustomed to survey in the past. Georgina was not a fool, nor inexperienced. She had comprehended at once in a general way, even if she did not look at the details, what odd and daunting components would make up this new future.

She saw already the long waits, the continuing loneliness, the aching frustration and worse fear, as well as the moments of thrill and happiness. She envisaged – and then thrust from her mind as trivial tiresomenesses – uncomfortable scenes with a procession of unsympathetic male figures: her lawyer and bank manager no doubt, her brother Simon certainly (Oh, *he* would never believe, she thought contemptuously), maybe eventually with someone at the War Office itself. She foresaw also delicate sessions with women friends and relations, who would appear sympathetic but would (oh yes, she knew) cluck and murmur disparagingly behind her back. They might even refer to her as 'poor Georgina'. They would speak of 'impostors' and 'temporary gentlemen' . . . Well, she was prepared for that. She was prepared for anything.

Norrie de la Foy at least would – surely? – be an ally. Together they would confront an unbelieving world. And they would win their sons back from the jaws of death –

But, no, she would not contact Norrie with the wonderful news just yet. The young man (Laurence, of course) had made her promise not to. And anyway . . . She found she wanted to nurse in her own mind this miraculous thing that had happened before communicating it even to Laurence's mother.

The great thing was to believe. She had been taught that from infancy. Faith could do everything – well, almost everything. There were genuine miracles. *Believe* . . . She clenched her fists. How lucky that she had always been a determined person. She had a number of times in the past year – she admitted it now – been tempted to abandon belief, to turn from the Presence. Oh yes, her Faith had been tested. But now it would triumph. With her Faith she would achieve what very few people could achieve; Raymond himself, in some form or shape, albeit only for fleeting moments, would be given back to her.

In a state close to ecstasy she sat on before her untouched meal facing the sunny, empty lawns.

Nothing Momentous

Years later, long after he was dead, he began to re-enter her dreams. She did not so much dream 'about' him as find herself momentarily back in the atmosphere of ease and happy expectation that was associated with him. He was somewhere there, in these dreams, but, as in life, not always within her range of vision, or in the same room with her. She only became sure that the other person in the dreams really was him, and not David or Timmy or someone else, when she saw his distinctively light grey eyes, with their flecked irises, smile at her at close quarters. In her dream, she felt so glad that he was still there – and then thought at once: of course he's still there. How could I ever have imagined he might not be?

These dreams did not come very often, not as often as she would have liked. There was nothing momentous about them. A daily relationship in which you constantly do things for the other person, and he for you, is not normally momentous in any way that can be crystallised in an event, or in a remembered word or gesture or embrace. It was the very casual, secure nature of the whole thing that came back to her in dreams as a fleeting essence, like a whiff of preserved emotion that has been concentrated and distilled and which, when released, is, like a scent, intense but fugitive, a hint rather than a fulfilment.

In the dreams they were, she thought, in the old house: that was why she felt so sure about everything, and did not necessarily need to be beside him to know he was there, going about the place whistling, or busy with something in his basement workshop, or stirring a pan of scrambled eggs in the kitchen, or sitting at his desk under his green-shaded lamp correcting exercise books or writing letters in his clear, deliberate, schoolmaster's hand. She did not dream precisely of these things, but waking memory supplied them. It supplied, too, early one morning, a previously mislaid image of the way in which the light of the lamp caught the curve of his cheek and the line of his hair, so that he looked, in that place, like the young man whom in fact she had never known.

Thus did dreams provoke memory and memories, in turn, supplement the dreams. And the emotion associated with him generalised, faintly but benignly, to her present life: on waking, she did not feel sad that the past was, after all, the past and would not return, but, rather, reassured that it was in some sense still real, still at work within her. And because, in dreams, locales are not distinct but can overlap and merge, like transparencies, the old house where he still was apparently to be found seemed to be fused to some extent with the house she and David and Timmy now shared; so that she would have been hard put to say where exactly the dreams were taking place and whether the house of her childhood and that of her married life were not, after all, one and the same thing.

In opaque, limited reality, however, the old house no longer existed: it had been pulled down – oh, fifteen or twenty years ago, probably, during that time when people were particularly busy destroying the past. Once, in the intervening years, she and David had gone by the end of the street in their car on some unremembered journey, and she had realised just in time and had cried out 'Oh, look – ' But there had been nothing left to look at. No houses any more, except for the pub at the end. Just an expanse of mown but littered grass and a row of saplings wilting in the urban sunlight, a manufactured oasis more hallucinatory and unconvincing than any dream-landscape.

But that experience had not roused him from the dead for her, because – she now remembered – Timmy had at that time been a small baby and she had been nursing him, and he in turn had protected her against everyone and every-thing, blotting out past and future in the present intensity of his needs. What a happy time that had been.

Timmy was tall now, and would never again need her very much. She did not grieve. They had had Timmy's

158

childhood, and it had been good. If you *had* something –
really had it, and it worked – then surely it was perverse to
mourn for it afterwards? She tried to say this once to David,
but he did not seem entirely convinced. David, she knew,
did not like losing things. He had not had as much practice
at it as she had. His own family home was still extant, every
room with its compliment of photographs, every cupboard
still filled with the accumulated evidence of several life-
times. Both his parents, though old, were still alive.

She remembered how, in her late childhood, it had
seemed odd to her that other people still had their mothers.
She knew of course in theory that it was the normal thing to
have one at her age, but in practice she could not imagine
what her own vaguely-remembered mother could contri-
bute to the life she and Daddy led. There would be nothing
much for her to do: she would just be in the way . . .

Every Saturday she and Daddy planned the meals for the
next week and did the main shop together at Sainsbury's.
On Sundays they cleaned the house, taking turns with the
Hoover as they both enjoyed that more than dusting. On
Sunday evenings Daddy took the washing to the
launderette, and she used to iron it on Monday or Tuesday
when she got in from school. She liked ironing: the growing
pile of soft, smooth shirts – his, mostly, with a couple of her
own school ones – gave her a sense of warm, peaceful
achievement. Any other food they needed during the week
he used to get on the way home from his own school. He was
usually in by five, unless he had a parents' meeting in the
evening, and when she had finished her homework he used
to read aloud to her – Arthur Ransome and Kipling. Later
Dickens and Hardy. However busy he was, he always had
time for that.

Once he said to her, 'You know, we're lucky: if I was in any
other job I probably wouldn't be home till about half-past six
or seven.' She recalled her faint incredulity at this information, and the daunting intimation it brought her that he was
not, after all, entirely in control of their joint destiny. She had
still been young enough, then, to believe that he was totally
powerful, above all rules made by other people.

159

On Friday evenings they used to go together to the early house at the cinema – there were so many cinemas and, it seemed, enjoyable films in those days – and then buy a fish-and-chip supper on the way home. After the fish, they used to have chocolate cake and then cheese, and Daddy used to have a glass or two of wine. Once she had turned thirteen, he let her have one, too. It was their weekly treat, a regular, private celebration of something never specifically expressed between them.

One evening, as they sat in front of the television, she suddenly said: 'I wish we went to the cinemas more. Now that Timmy is old enough to entertain himself . . .'

David looked slightly surprised:

'Well, we do go sometimes, don't we? But there's no point unless there's a good film on, and often there's something better on the box anyway. Don't you remember on your birthday looking all through the list of *What's On*, and there was nothing but that French film we'd already seen or that one about Poland you didn't want to see, or else sex 'n' violence? We counted, and well over *half* the cinemas had on rubbish like *Sexy Susan Sins Again*. Or worse.'

'What could be worse than that?' she said, laughing, but feeling obscurely irritated. He did not specify.

She remembered with forebearing – oh, it was years ago now – her naïve consternation when, early on in their marriage, she had found by chance a colourful magazine tucked away in his brief case. Of course magazines like that weren't as commonplace then as they had since become. She had recoiled from some of the pictures, and then, when he had found her brooding, had admitted why. He had been embarrassed, touched, and a shade over-emphatic:

'Darling, that sort of thing is ordinary and quite harmless – honestly. I know it doesn't appeal to a woman like you. I wouldn't expect it to, but believe me there's nothing nasty about it. I don't go one bit for the harder stuff – paedophilia, snuff movies, that sort of thing. That would seem to me as repulsive as it would to you.'

David was a social worker. Not one of the Marxist,

society-is-to-blame sort (as he always assured new acquaintances) but one of the down-to-earth, cynical sort that clients
actually trusted more. She knew, however, that he was
more entranced by his job, and perhaps more gullible, than
he pretended to be. Sitting at home with the television, they
watched programmes about single mothers and unmarried
fathers, about child abuse and Granny-battering, about
incest, bereavement, handicaps, sickness, guilt, unemploy-
ment and identity crises, criminality, bestiality and death.
Sometimes, watching her husband's calm face outlined
against the light from the screen, she wondered if he were
really as compassionately unshockable as he seemed. She
had never put the matter to the test.

It had been after a programme on bereavement not long
ago that she had said to him:

'You know, it puzzles me a bit . . . that I didn't sort of
notice more when Daddy died.'

He looked at her carefully, as if uncertain what she might
mean.

'It was when we were in the North,' he said at last. 'You
hadn't seen him for months, hardly at all much for two
years, in fact. And Timmy was small. You did cry a lot,
though, when your Auntie Susan rang up and told you.'

'Of course I did. It was such a shock. That wasn't quite
what I meant. It was as if I didn't really *feel* his going. Or
even have any sense that he had gone. It was more just as if –
I hadn't seen him lately. It stayed that way for years . . .'

'Well, love, he did do his best to slip away without you
feeling it, didn't he? All that going into hospital without
even telling us, and then giving directions there wasn't to be
a funeral or anything. He was such a nice man, I'm sure he
did it with the best of intentions – wanting to spare you. But
sometimes I wondered . . .' He did not finish the sentence,
and she, scenting possible criticism, did not encourage him
to.

Later, one night, it occurred to her that she had asked the
wrong question. It was not so very surprising (as David
said) that his death had not made a proper impression on
her, given the circumstances. What was more surprising

161

was that those circumstances should have developed at all. In the loving backwash of another dream, deeply penetrated by memory, she suddenly asked herself:

How did I ever come to leave him?

It was not remorse she felt, but simple incomprehension. It was as if some brief but very significant bit of the past were blotted out, and she could not now recapture even the sequence of practical events that had carried her away from Daddy, let alone their meaning. True, she had gone away to college: he had always expected her to do that . . . And there she had met David. Had he expected her to do that too? Possibly. And a really loving parent (David would give this little lecture any time if asked, and occasionally when not asked) is one who is unselfishly prepared to let his child go when the time is ready. But this, as an explanation of what had actually taken place, was entirely inadequate. It wasn't – couldn't have been? – as simple as that. Nothing like.

She must, she thought, have been very innocent at nineteen or twenty. She did not seem to have grasped, till it was all done and settled and irrevocable, that one love may – must? – overshadow and gradually exclude another. Plumbing uncertainly the reaches of her memory (she had never had a very good memory) it seemed to her that there had been no conflict in her mind because she had made no distinction between the one love and the other. Loving David had been just like an extension of what she had already experienced, an enlargement, not a change. Ideas such as 'loyalty', 'loss', 'betrayal' or even 'decision' did not impinge upon her consciousness. Helplessly and indestructibly female, she had let life carry her on its own momentum.

One morning she said to David with a touch of desperation in her voice:

'I wonder why I keep dreaming about him, though? After all these years . . .' David did not, by this time, need to ask who 'he' was. He said after a pause:

'Perhaps it's your age.'

'Oh, don't be so silly.'

162

'I'm not being silly. I just mean that you must, now, be about the age he was when you remember him best. Aren't you?'

'Yes. Yes, I suppose I am.'

'There you are,' said the social worker triumphantly. 'We all have our parents as models to some extent. You were very close to him when he was around forty. Now you're getting on for forty yourself your subconscious is dredging him up and looking at him – if you'll excuse the phrase.'

She let it pass. She did not, in fact, think that David was right. She did not believe, now, that her father had even been buried – or submerged – whatever the harsh word 'dredge' implied. She thought he had been there in her life all the time, like someone who just happens to be in another room, only she had been too busy, all those years of Timmy's childhood, to take proper account of the fact. Now Timmy was growing up, it was as if she had dried her hands on a towel and turned round to see her father entering the room, casually, pipe in hand, smiling, undisplaced by death or anything else.

In her dreams, he never came nearer to her than that. What bound them indissolubly to each other was only a hint, the essence extracted from concentrated, irreducible feeling . . . She both longed and dreaded that one of these nights he would once again come nearer to her, as he had in life.

She remembered now, in loving, obsessional detail, his brown hair that was just touched with grey, his lined, serious face, his young, light, smiling eyes. She remembered the pores in his skin, close up, and thinking how funny a man's skin and smell was, quite different from one's own. She remembered his fine, well-shaped hands with their gold signet-ring that Mummy had given him when they had got married, and how those hands looked against her own white skin, against her inconsequential, half-developed breasts. She remembered – in a rush of vertiginous recall – those same hands holding her, parting her legs, touching her, teaching her, cherishing her. She remembered how overwhelmingly, disarmingly gentle and patient he had been: she even recalled – though she could not hear the words he spoke – the reassuring tone of his voice, his extreme tenderness.

It had all been so simple, so natural and, in the end, so easy. It had never once occurred to her to recoil from him or reject him. How could she be frightened or upset, whatever he did? It was so clear that he loved her and wanted only good for her.

If she had told no one, ever, about what they had shared, that was simply because, as Daddy had said to her, it was too private and special to be discussed with other people.

Yet now the orphaned woman waited for this loved ghost to invade her bed with a certain dread. It was not him she feared – poor, neglected ghost, poor darling, poor Daddy. It was what that ghost might raise within herself and what she herself might do in consequence. She lay beside her sleeping husband, and was alone.